BUTTERFLY LADY

Jan had a consuming passion for flowers. She photographed them, painted them, and sold them in her florist shop in the beautiful mountain country east of Cape Town. One day, Jan decides to make the long drive to see a field of the famous Namaqualand daisies, and there she has a chance encounter with a handsome stranger that changes her whole life. Love blossoms between Jan and Raoul Jourdan, the owner of a large vineyard — until she realises he could have been responsible for her father's death.

Books by Beverley Winter
in the Linford Romance Library:

HOUSE ON THE HILL
A TIME TO LOVE
LOVE UNDERCOVER
MORTIMER HONOUR
THE HEART'S LONGING
LOVE ON SAFARI
WOMAN WITH A MISSION

BEVERLEY WINTER

BUTTERFLY LADY

Complete and Unabridged

LINFORD
Leicester

First published in Great Britain in 2003

First Linford Edition
published 2004

British Library CIP Data

Winter, Beverley
    Butterfly lady.—Large print ed.—
Linford romance library
    1. Romantic suspense novels
    2. Large type books
    I. Title
    823.9′14 [F]

    ISBN 1–84395–536–9

Published by
F. A. Thorpe (Publishing)
Anstey, Leicestershire

Set by Words & Graphics Ltd.
Anstey, Leicestershire
Printed and bound in Great Britain by
T. J. International Ltd., Padstow, Cornwall

This book is printed on acid-free paper

1

Jan Harding wound down the window of her car, removed her dark glasses and stared at the scene in awe.

'Oh, wow!'

As far as the eye could see stretched a tangled profusion of blossoms which carpeted the land in pink, yellow and fiery orange. It was a miracle of nature which had transformed the rocky, rather barren landscape into a floral wonderland. The famous Namaqualand daisies which appeared each spring after the winter rains had cooled and soaked the scorched earth were indeed everything the guidebook had promised, and worth every moment of the long drive she'd made in order to view them.

Flowers were Jan's consuming passion. She photographed them, painted them, pressed them, dried them, bought them and sold them, mostly at her little florist-cum-craft shop, Jan's Blooms. The business was situated in the beautiful mountain country east of Cape Town where the university town of Stellenbosch nestled beside the river. It was the town of her birth, and a major centre of the wine and fruit industry in South Africa, known for its beautiful, stately houses and ancient avenues of oak trees.

Jan grabbed her camera from the seat beside her and climbed out of the car, thankful at last to be able to stretch her long, jeans-clad legs. It had been a hot, tedious drive and she could do with a can of juice, but first things first — the photographs!

A cooling breeze wafted a delightful floral scent against her cheeks and fanned her long fair hair across her face. Impatiently she reached into the interior of the car for a scarf to fasten its thick strands into a pony tail so that they didn't obscure the lens at the wrong moment.

It seemed a pity to disturb the butterflies, but she had work to do. With a little thrill of delight she waded carefully into the breeze-tossed multi-coloured carpet and paused for a moment in concentration. Then with careful deliberation Jan began to take her photographs, intent on getting the best possible shots while the light remained. Hopefully the pictures would be good enough to frame and offer for sale in her shop.

She was so intent on her work that she failed to notice where she was going, until something large and solid connected with her right foot. With a squeal of alarm, Jan lost her balance and pitched forward as her precious, state-of-the-art camera rolled away into the daisies. A moment later she found herself in a contorted, undignified heap, right on top of a large, hard male body!

'What the heck are you doing, you crazy woman?' a deep, furious voice rumbled. 'Watch where you're going next time. You scared the bejabbers out of me.'

Jan lifted her head and stared in horror at the owner of the voice. Her heart was spinning so fiercely it had somersaulted into her throat, and what breath she had left came in great, terrified gasps. In order to hide her fear, she resorted to anger, a defence mechanism she'd learned to employ when feeling threatened. Any crazy person lying in wait for people in a lonely field deserved the sharp edge of her tongue.

'You're the dumb idiot, not me!' she snapped. 'I bet that if they put your brain inside a grasshopper it would most probably hop backwards.'

'Oh, yeah?'

'Yeah,' Jan taunted and added sassily, 'grasshopper man.'

A strong pair of arms tightened convulsively around her body, pinning her to a vast, solid chest.

'Say that again,' he commanded with amusement, 'butterfly lady!'

If Jan's heart had been performing circus tricks a moment before, it was nothing compared to the way it was behaving now. The only consolation was that his own heart appeared to be thudding just as frantically. It reminded her of a stampeding herd of buffalo!

'Let me go, or I'll scream!' she quavered, her fear returning in a rush.

His hard, muscular arms were like a vice trying to contain a quivering jelly. In a moment she'd disintegrate completely, and it would all be his fault! Blimey, the man was so strong.

'Scream away, lady,' he drawled.

His eyes were fastened intently on her flushed face and she could feel his warm, minty breath on her cheeks. Embarrassed at finding herself in such close proximity to a perfect stranger, Jan began to struggle.

'Keep still,' the man growled. 'I wish to take a look at the butterfly I've caught.'

Furiously, Jan glared back, dismayed to find that her usual calm had completely deserted her. Her stupid heart would not stop lurching against her ribs, perhaps because what she saw and felt both frightened and excited her. This, she thought wildly, was the man she'd been waiting for!

His grey eyes were so light they were almost iridescent, heavily lashed and lazily veiled as they deliberately examined each of her features in turn.

'Hm. A rather beautiful butterfly, it seems.'

His eyes held hers for a long, thoughtful moment before seeking her mouth. Afraid that he would take it into his handsome head to kiss her, Jan panicked.

'Don't even think about it!' she hissed.

He ignored her, deliberately placing one large hand behind her head and urging her forward until he was able to brush her lips with his own. Then taking his time, he proceeded to kiss her rather more thoroughly.

'Mm. Not bad, for a butterfly,' he said.

He'd felt her shiver when he'd kissed her, and it had jolted him, set his pulse racing even faster. A moment earlier he'd been dreaming of butterflies, and then one had materialised in the flesh. He must have died and gone to heaven!

'How dare you!' Jan retorted when her breath returned. 'You shouldn't have done that.'

His eyebrows rose.

'I thought it was what you'd been hoping for.'

Jan blushed scarlet. He must be a mind reader!

The man appeared to be in his thirties, with looks good enough to turn even the most blasé of female heads. His hair was very dark and fashionably short with attractive silver streaks threading the temples. There was a tiny scar on one cheekbone and his dark stubble had at least two days' growth. In another age he would have been a pirate!

Jan became aware that she was staring, mesmerised by those strange, twinkling eyes. What's more, her mouth had fallen open. She closed it with a snap.

'I said, let me go,' she commanded fiercely, disconcerted to find that her voice had lost its usual husky modulation and sounded like a shrew, sharp with tension.

To her amazement, he immediately relaxed his hold.

'Certainly.'

He then added, 'Feel free to fall upon me any time, butterfly lady.'

Jan gave an unladylike snort. Anyone would think she'd done it deliberately! And she wished he wouldn't refer to her as a butterfly. It made her feel like a dizzy, little bimbo when in reality she was a mature, creative twenty-four-year-old with diplomas in art and floristry.

Trying to remain dignified, she heaved herself off his chest, scrambled to her feet and carefully inspected her grazed palms. They weren't too bad. With a stony expression she bent to retrieve her camera. No damage done there, either, thank goodness.

'Ah,' the man mocked, 'one of those snap-happy tourists, come to see the sights.'

'What's wrong with that?' Jan retorted. 'It's a beautiful sight.'

'Did I say it wasn't?'

She looked down her straight little nose and scowled.

'Your own presence here is highly suspect, I'll have you know. One doesn't expect to find a hulking, great weirdo lurking amongst the wild flowers. You should be ashamed of yourself, lying in wait for an innocent woman.'

There was a strangled sound, like hastily-suppressed laughter. Then, despite his size, the man sprang up with masculine grace and unfolded himself to an immense height. Jan's wide-eyed gaze took in every detail of his appearance. He was what her grandmother would have called a fine figure of a man — tall and tanned and well-honed. She was tall herself, but at this rate she'd need a stepladder to look him in the eye!

He was wearing a once-white T-shirt which looked fit for the garbage, together with a pair of running shoes, and his grubby black shorts were positively indecent, moulding his strong, muscular thighs like a second skin. He might cut a very fine figure but he had absolutely no idea about dress! Perhaps, she thought without pity, he was nearing his last cent.

The man stared back from a bland face, his eyes gleaming with amusement as he narrowed them against the afternoon glare. Jan examined his features, curiosity overcoming her natural reserve. He had dark brows, a straight nose and a tough jaw which hinted at a ruthless determination. His mouth, firm and turned up at the ends, appeared to be suppressing a leer.

She glanced nervously over her shoulder only to discover she'd rambled some way from her car. Supposing he made another pass? She wouldn't be able to run very fast because her ankle was beginning to ache. She must have wrenched it when she'd fallen.

'Relax, butterfly lady,' he mocked.

His voice was deep and gravelly, which did nothing to allay her fears, rasping in her ears.

'Allow me to explain that I'm not into seducing strange damsels who hurl themselves at me on a hot day.'

'I was not hurling myself at you,' Jan told him furiously. 'I was simply taking a few photographs when I happened to trip, and why you were lying there anyway is beyond anyone's comprehension!'

He viewed her pityingly.

'Then I'll enlighten you. I was taking a nap.'

'In the middle of the daisies?'

'Why not? I was tired.'

Jan thought she had never met such an odd individual. The sooner she put some distance between them, the better. It was an isolated place and as he had already insinuated, there would be nobody to hear her screams.

'Well, goodbye,' she told him quickly, trying not to sound as nervous as she felt, and turned sharply on her heel.

Unfortunately it was the wrong heel. With a small sound of distress, she sank into the daisies, pain lancing through her like a hot knife. Immediately, the mockery disappeared, to be replaced by a look of concern.

'You've injured yourself,' he said quietly.

He was beside her in a second, his large hands probing her lower leg and ankle bone very gently.

'A slight sprain, I think. It's definitely not broken, anyway. Wait here.'

Since she couldn't very well do anything else, Jan waited, tense with fear. She was completely at his mercy and it wasn't a good feeling. Her gaze followed his tall figure as it strode purposefully through the blossoms. To her amazement, he stooped down to retrieve a cycle hidden amongst them, and opened a black bag attached to its saddle.

'May I?'

With surprising deftness he fastened a crêpe bandage around her ankle, securing it expertly with an elasticised clip.

'Can you put your weight on your ankle?' he asked.

'Yes, I think so. I'll try.'

With a small yelp of pain, Jan gazed at him helplessly. Without another word, he bent to lift her as though she weighed little more than a doll. He held her against him and carried her to her car where he deposited her gently on the driver's seat.

'Do you think you can manage? The injury doesn't look too serious but you'd be advised to have that ankle X-rayed when you get home. Goodbye, Miss . . . er . . . '

'Harding,' she told him reluctantly.

Her heart was in her throat again. He really was the oddest, most scary male she'd ever met. She remembered her manners and added quickly, 'Thank you for your help. I do appreciate it, honestly.'

'No problem, Miss Harding. Drive carefully.'

He sketched a casual salute and turned back into the daisies. The last view Jan had of him was through her rear view mirror. He wheeled his cycle out on to the road, fastened on a helmet, hefted one muscular leg over the saddle and peddled away effort-lessly.

'Well!' she exploded in frustration.

Whoever he was, he'd certainly spoiled her afternoon!

She put the car into gear and gingerly released the clutch. With her left ankle on fire she had no idea how she was going to make it all the way back to her home. After ten minutes, Jan decided rather reluctantly that driving was too painful. She would have to find overnight accommodation and continue with her journey in the morning. She drove on steadily to the nearest town, scarcely aware of the attractive scenery, glancing only vaguely at the fertile valleys filled with orange groves. Some happier day, Jan promised herself, she would return to the area and tour the groves.

The small town which hove into view boasted one small hotel. With a thankful sigh, Jan parked before its gabled front and hobbled into the reception area. There were a number of luxury coaches in the adjacent carpark, obviously used to transport tourists who were en route to view the area's wild flower displays, as she had done.

To her dismay, the receptionist was not very helpful.

'The coach tours book rooms well in advance, you know,' she told Jan pointedly. 'Unfortunately, we do not have a single one left.'

'I see. Thank you.'

Unable to hide her disappointment, Jan turned away. The sun was going down, she was hot, weary and miserable, and now she was forced to press on to the next town. She went into the lounge and ordered a long, cool drink, taking her time about it as she rested her foot for as long as she could. When eventually she left, the receptionist, taking pity, called after her.

'Why don't you try one of the nearby farms? There are one or two farther along the road which offer a bed-and-breakfast service.'

Jan brightened.

'Yes, I think I will. Thanks.'

She limped painfully back to the car, fired the engine and drove quickly through the town. Dusk had settled by the time she came to a turn-off bearing a hopeful sign — **Citrusdale. Bed and Breakfast**.

Feeling profoundly relieved, Jan negotiated the dusty farm road. Not long now. The road gave on to a broad sweep of gravel in front of a large, whitewashed homestead surrounded by shrub-dotted lawns. A child's swing hung from one of the trees and one or two lights twinkled a welcome through the open windows. Somewhere in the background came the laughter of children. It seemed like a nice welcoming, family home.

Two yellow Labradors came bounding up to investigate her arrival as she climbed from the driving seat, in too much pain to be afraid of their deep-throated barks.

'Well, I'll be darned.'

Jan stiffened at the deep, familiar voice which came out of the dusk behind her. It was that man again. What appalling luck! Anyone would think it had been written in the stars. She glared at him in disbelief.

'I didn't expect to find you here.'

The man inclined his head.

'Likewise. Good evening, butterfly lady.'

He'd changed out of his disreputable clothing into a clean pair of jeans and a crisp, open-necked shirt, and his hair was still damp from the shower. He'd shaved, too, Jan noticed with a small tripling of her heart rate. It took away his earlier rakish air, replacing it with a certain suave sophistication. If anything, it was even more intimidating.

He laughed softly.

'I'm on to you, you know. You followed me here, didn't you? You're persistent, I'll give you that.'

Jan was outraged.

'What a rude, conceited man you are. I had no idea you lived here, and I certainly won't stay to be insulted!'

She turned around, intent on making a quick getaway. Nothing would induce her to stay under this man's roof, even for one night. She would try the next farm, but a large hand clamped her arm.

'Not so fast. Relax, butterfly lady, there is no need to rush away. I may have misjudged the situation. Maybe your arrival here is sheer coincidence, after all.'

Jan tried to pull her arm away, but his grip tightened.

'What exactly do you want?' he asked.

'Not you,' she taunted, and was pleased to see the thinning of his lips. 'I came to ask for a room for the night because I can't travel much farther with this ankle.'

To her utter mortification, her voice faded into a wobble. She stared up at him with large eyes, unable to hide the fatigue, anger and pain in them. Wordlessly, he stooped and collected her into his arms.

'Hey, put me down!'

Ignoring her plea, he carried her up the front steps and across the colonnaded veranda, shouldering his way through the sturdy front door.

'Raoul,' a lifting female voice called from within, 'who is it?'

A pretty, petite young woman with dark hair bustled into the hallway. Her eyes widened.

'My goodness, brother, dear, what have we here?'

'An injured butterfly.'

He pushed open the door leading to the living-room and deposited Jan on to a squashy pink sofa.

'This,' he explained, not removing his eyes from Jan's face, 'is Miss Harding, whom I met earlier today. It appears that she requires accommodation at Citrusdale.'

'Oh, no problem,' the woman said and smiled. 'I'm Antoinette De Villiers, Raoul's sister. What a mercy you arrived this evening, and not tomorrow. I can let you have a room, for one night only, but I need it for guests from Cape Town tomorrow evening. Will that do?'

She named a fee and Jan summoned a tight smile.

'One night is all I need, thank you, and I'll leave after breakfast in the morning. I'm afraid I don't have any luggage with me. I was expecting to return to my home this evening, but I've injured my ankle and find it difficult to drive. The hotel in one of the towns I drove through advised me to try a farm along this road.'

'A good thing, too, Miss Harding.'
She smiled sympathetically.

'You need to rest that ankle. May I suggest that you get straight into bed? I'll bring you a tray later on. Would you like to borrow a nightdress?'

Gratefully, Jan accepted. What a kind woman she was, unlike her unspeakable brother, who appeared to be finding amusement in the situation.

'Come along to bed, then, Miss Harding,' he invited without bothering to hide his grin. 'It seems I'm to be lumbered with you for the next twelve hours.'

Once more he lifted her effortlessly and strode down the passage to a pretty blue and white bedroom which over-looked an orange grove.

'Thank you,' Jan said shortly as he lowered her to the bed, then she added dismissively. 'You can go, now Mister . . . er . . .'

'The name is Jourdan, Raoul Jourdan.'

Despite his obvious South African accent, he pronounced it like a Frenchman.

'Whatever,' Jan muttered under her breath.

She couldn't care less who the heck he was. Her ankle was on fire and she'd had enough of being bundled about like one of his sacks of oranges. Raoul Jourdan hooked his thumbs into the pockets of his jeans and regarded her thoughtfully.

'Where is your home?'

Jan leaned back against the spotless, lace-edged pillows and glared at him. She had no intention of being interrogated by this cock-sure, self-satisfied man. Why didn't he go away and leave her in peace?

'That is hardly any of your business,' she retorted.

Her gaze dropped to his wide shoulders and then to the muscular forearms which held a sprinkling of crisp, dark hair. One wrist sported an expensive gold watch which gleamed richly against his tanned skin. He was obviously not quite the pauper she'd first imagined.

'That's a matter of opinion, my dear.'

'I am not your dear,' Jan snapped.

'No, but you will be.'

Jan gasped.

'I beg your pardon?'

'I said, you will be. Just remember that.'

She stared at the closed door, completely bereft of words. It was all too much! With a sniff she closed her eyes on the two small tears which were squeezing their way between her lashes.

Apart from the flowers, it had been a beastly day, and now this unhinged individual of French descent was making incomprehensible threats about her future. It was so ludicrous that if she wasn't feeling so miserable at this moment, she'd be laughing her head off.

His dear, indeed! She'd rather fall in love with a grasshopper.

2

Jan's Blooms occupied small, elongated premises next to a tea garden in one of the quieter streets of Stellenbosch. The rented building was old, with timbered floors and rough-cast, whitewashed walls, but in Jan's estimation it had that precious commodity — atmosphere.

Various articles ranging from pottery jars filled with dried lavender to handcrafted knitwear and colourful batik prints occupied the wide, wooden shelves. The walls boasted tasteful, floral pictures of varying description, paintings, photographs and gilt-framed miniatures of pressed flowers.

On display in the front of the shop were large vases of fresh flowers, with one or two artfully made-up arrangements occupying the front window. Hard at work in the back room, preparing more floral arrangements, was Clare Tatham, Jan's part-time assistant. She glanced up when Jan entered and hung up her keys on the board beside the back door.

'Jan! What happened? It's not like you to be late.'

Jan smiled ruefully.

'Car trouble, Clare. Fan belt. I had to go to the garage, which was a nuisance, but I knew you were more than able to hold the fort here. Have you been busy?'

'Not particularly. I've made up those two orders we took on Friday, and the woman said she'll call for them at twelve.'

She paused, eyeing Jan's foot in concern.

'You're limping.'

Jan made light of her predicament.

'Oh, it's nothing drastic. I fell over in a field. The ankle is still a little swollen, but much better than it was. When I got home yesterday I packed it with ice and took it easy for the rest of the day. I'll be fine by tomorrow.'

The week sped by. On Thursday, Jan bought fresh flowers from the wholesaler at the crack of dawn, drove them to the shop and arranged them to the satisfaction and delight of her various customers. She had a regular following of housewives, too, who returned time and again to buy fresh flowers for their own floral arrangements.

During the evenings, Jan worked at home. She framed the photographs she'd taken the previous weekend and tie-dyed more batik prints, intending to make them into cushion covers at a later date. On Friday evening, she prepared a new canvas for painting. She rather fancied a scene with arum lilies in a field.

On Saturday morning, Jan urged Clare to hurry home early, knowing that her friend wished to prepare for her small daughter's birthday party. The busy period was over and she could easily man the shop alone until closing time. As she filled the buckets with fresh water in readiness for her trip to the flower market early on Monday morning, Jan's thoughts drifted to her strange experience of the previous weekend.

There had scarcely been a day that she had not thought about the enigmatic stranger she'd met amongst the daisies. He was the most disturbing man she'd ever encountered, and to her immense frustration she could not get him out of her mind. How clearly she remembered the feel of him, a safe, solid feeling.

With a small sound of exasperation Jan re-focused her thoughts on the arrangement of silk flowers she was busy with. The man was becoming a threat to her peace of mind! It was just as well she would never see him again. She reached for her wire cutters and snipped the end off a pink rosebud, pressing the stalk absently into the creamy oasis which formed the base of the arrangement. The next rosebud received the same treatment, followed by a branch of grey-green florist's gum.

Lavender. She needed some dried lavender. Jan put down her cutters, intending to fetch it, but immediately lost herself in thought. The expression on Raoul Jourdan's silver grey eyes had not been difficult to interpret as he'd delivered his parting shot from the doorway of the farm bedroom.

'You will be.'

There had been admiration, mockery, tenderness, flinty determination.

With a sigh, Jan rose from her stool behind the workbench. At this rate she would never get any work done!

Just before closing time the doorbell pinged. About to replace the jar of lavender on the shelf, Jan looked up enquiringly. To her utter astonishment she encountered once more the mixture of admiration, mockery, tenderness and flinty determination! Raoul Jourdan was leaning casually against the doorframe, his smile mocking.

'Good afternoon, butterfly lady.'

Jan's breath locked in her chest. She

swallowed convulsively.

'What . . . what do you want?' and before he could reply she said crossly, 'And I am not a butterfly. My name is Jan.'

'Yes, I know. It's written outside plainly for all to see — **Jan's Blooms**.'

'But how did you know where to find me?'

The light eyes gleamed with amusement.

'I phoned every Harding in the book. I'm looking for a lady with a passion for flowers, I told them. It was a long shot, but eventually I struck gold. Your grandmother was a fount of information.'

Jan gaped.

'But why would you do such a thing? You're impossible!'

He stood gazing at her, in no seeming hurry to be about his business.

Finally she snapped, 'What is it you want, Mister Jourdan?'

'Flowers.'

'What kind of flowers?'

'I need a number of arrangements for my home.'

'Well, you've come an awful long way to get them. Surely there's a florist shop closer to Citrusdale.'

'Citrusdale? Who said anything about Citrusdale? My sister is perfectly capable of finding her own flowers.'

'I don't understand.'

'I grow grapes, Miss Harding, not oranges.'

He straightened to his full height and sauntered into the shop.

'My home is near Franschhoek.'

Jan blinked.

'Oh. I see.'

French Glen — a beautiful valley surrounded by mountains, the land given to Protestant Huguenot refugees who had fled a Europe torn by religious strife in the seventeenth century. It was an area of splendid vineyards and gracious, period architecture, and Jan had been there only once. It had not been a happy occasion.

Marshalling her thoughts, she became

businesslike. The sooner she sorted out the man's problem, the sooner he would leave her in peace!

'Do you require anything in particular? Dried flowers or fresh? We have a considerable stock of silk blooms, should you prefer that. In fact we have some lovely designs already made up, if you'd care to see them.'

She indicated towards the back room.

'Come through, please, Mister Jourdan.'

'Raoul,' he said.

'Er, yes. Well, what is it you have in mind, Raoul?'

To her annoyance, he remained standing in the middle of the shop.

'I really have no idea. May I call you Jan? I can't tell a rose from a lily.'

Jan sighed.

'Surely you have some idea.'

'None at all. That's why I'm here.'

The light eyes surveyed her lazily, taking in every detail of her businesslike blouse and pencil-slim black skirt.

'I need you to come to my home and

see for yourself.'

Seeing her doubtful expression, he added quickly, 'The décor, you know. You would need to view the colour combinations. I wish the arrangements to be well co-ordinated. They must match the interiors. I'm not much good with that sort of thing. You, mademoiselle, will know precisely what is needed.'

'How many arrangements do you require?'

'That depends entirely upon you. Large or small, dried or fresh, one vase or ten, you need spare no cost. My home is large and gracious, and I want only the best.'

Jan's interest quickened. How could she resist such an offer? It would boost the coffers considerably. Besides, she had a treacherous, sneaking desire to see where he lived. If his home was in the Valley of the Huguenots, the chances were he'd live in one of those beautiful, old manor houses surrounded by ancient camphor trees. Not wishing to appear too eager, she pretended to consult her diary.

'I could come some time next week. Let me see.'

'What about today?'

She looked up sharply.

'Impossible. It's Saturday.'

'I'm in a hurry for those flowers.'

He glanced at his watch.

'It's nearly closing time, isn't it? I'll expect you in an hour's time. I'll show you around the place, we'll have a cup of coffee and then you shall tell me what you think.'

Jan could think of no excuse on the spur of the moment and agreed reluctantly.

'I am not too familiar with the area. You will have to give me the directions.'

'No problem, the estate is well sign-posted. It's called Sans Souci.'

Jan dropped her pen. Good grief, he was one of those Jourdans!

The first and last time she'd visited her father's office on that same estate, she'd vowed never to return. She'd been eight years old and it had been the only time she'd ever seen her father cry.

Raoul retrieved her pen and placed it on the counter.

He explained casually, 'Sans Souci means without care, you know. It's a peaceful place. We try to live up to its name.'

Well, you don't succeed, Jan thought furiously.

The owners of Sans Souci had been totally unconcerned that her father had lost all his money and died a broken man! He'd worked on the estate for years, a loyal and dedicated employee, and they'd kicked him in the teeth. They couldn't have cared less, in fact. The Jourdans were an unscrupulous, cold-hearted lot, and she wanted nothing to do with any of them. Jan took a deep breath.

She said coldly, 'I cannot take this assignment.'

Raoul's eyes narrowed.

'What do you mean, you cannot take the assignment? I'll make it worth your while, believe me.'

'It's not a question of money. It's a question of principle.'

'I don't understand.'

Jan smiled sweetly.

'No, you wouldn't, would you? You're a Jourdan.'

She indicated the door.

'I am closing my business now, sir, and must ask you to leave. Goodbye.'

★ ★ ★

Jan drove home to her small, rented cottage on the outskirts of the town. Her insides were all quivery, and the sooner she pulled herself together, the better. She parked in her usual place under the oak tree in the garden, near the small, paved patio which led off the living-room, a sun-trap where she relaxed on Saturday afternoons after her busy week.

'I'm home,' she called, tossing her keys into a dish on the hall table.

Tiger, her one-eyed tom cat with

frayed ears, appeared from the living-room and rubbed against her leg. At the same time her grandmother bustled through from the kitchen.

'There you are, Janetta. Had a good day, dear?'

Briefly Jan thought about it. It had been a good one until he'd shown up!

'Not too bad,' she murmured, summoning a small smile for her grandmother's benefit.

'I had the strangest phone call this morning,' the old lady told her. 'Someone wanting to find out about Jan's Blooms, said he was a prospective customer. A very charming man, and we chatted for ages. I gave him the address of the shop. Did he show up?'

'Yes.'

Quickly she changed the subject.

'What have you been doing with yourself, Grandmother?'

'Oh, the usual. I baked a seed cake, pottered round the garden and then took myself inside to practise the piano. Have to keep the old, arthritic fingers out of trouble, you know. It's amazing what a few scales will do for stiff joints, not to mention that Chopin nocturne.'

Jan kissed her grandmother's cheek.

'If I'm half as fit as you are when I'm your age, I'll be happy. I'll make us a macaroni cheese for supper, shall I?'

'No need. There's a chicken casserole in the oven. I felt energetic today.'

Jan smiled, genuinely this time.

'Great. Then what about a cup of tea? Go and sit on the patio while I cut two chunks of seed cake, Gran. I'm starving.'

Her grandmother was a dear, and the only surviving member of her family. After her father's suicide, the two of them had turned to each other for comfort, moving into the small cottage which Grandmother had rented from her meagre pension. Once Jan was old enough to assume responsibility for the household finances, they had fared rather better, but it had not been easy. It was only recently that Jan's business had really started to prosper, and she could give her grandmother the little treats she deserved.

Her father's death had dealt them a difficult blow. It was all a long time ago, but the hurt remained. At the time it had all been incomprehensible to a young child, but as she'd grown older she'd tried to rationalise the situation. Losing all his money so soon after her mother's death must have driven her father over the edge, Jan reflected sadly.

It would not do to let Grandmother see how unsettled she was feeling so with a determinedly carefree air she carried the tray out to the patio and poured their tea into the dainty china cups her grandmother had always favoured.

'Much nicer in proper cups,' the old lady commented as she savoured her first sip. 'And grown right here in the Cape, too. It's refreshing, isn't it? It reminds me, 'there's many a slip 'twixt the cup and the lip'.'

Jan hid a grin. Here it came — the maxim of the day! Her grandmother was exceedingly fond of quoting proverbs, and the fact that they were often out of context did not trouble the old lady in the slightest.

'Meaning?'

'Well, don't take anything for granted, dear.'

'And what am I supposed to be taking for granted, Grandmother, dear?'

'The fact that I'll be around here for ever. You must find yourself a husband, Janetta. I've been giving it a lot of thought lately. We must contrive to buy you a new wardrobe, and perhaps you could take one or two tours, meet new people.'

Jan put down her cup and stared at the old lady in amazement.

'And what, may I ask, has brought on this sudden fit of thinking?'

Her grandmother fixed her with a stern eye.

'You know as well as I do that I'm not a particularly well woman, Janetta. The old ticker, the old blood pressure, and so on. I should like to see you settled, child, before I join your grandfather.'

Jan choked on her seed cake.

'Grandmother, you are not to talk like that!'

'Why not?' the old lady asked calmly. 'I believe in calling a spade a spade. You were a lonely little girl and I should not like you to be a lonely, old woman, which you will be, if nothing is done to remedy matters.'

'You speak as though finding a husband is like going into the supermarket and choosing a bottle of wine. What shall I have?' Jan mimicked. 'A good Chardonnay from the L'Avenir Estate?'

Her grandmother chuckled.

'Why not make it a Special Late Harvest from Sans Souci?'

Jan started, so that her tea sloshed all over the saucer.

'What is it, dear? Do you not favour Sans Souci wines?' the old lady asked in consternation.

Jan took a deep breath.

'I have never sampled them.'

What's more, I never will, she said to herself.

'No? Oh, my dear, you are missing something wonderful. I'll tell you what we shall do. We shall take a drive out to the Sans Souci estate next Saturday afternoon and visit the cellar there. We'll treat ourselves, and I shall buy a bottle of their Chenin Blanc. It's out of this world.'

'Chenin Blanc from Sans Souci,' Jan muttered disbelievingly. 'Heaven preserve us.'

The old lady misunderstood her reluctance.

'You'll love it, Jan. It's an elegant, off-dry white, you know, with a crisp, fruity flavour. We'll pop a chicken in the oven before we go, and I'll make one of my fruit tarts for dessert.'

Jan took a deep breath.

'Are you sure you want to do this, Grandmother?'

'Of course. It's pension day on Friday and I shall be rich.'

Her grandmother had so few pleasures left to her that Jan hadn't the heart to refuse. However, with any luck she'd have forgotten all about it by next Saturday.

However, Daffodil Burney did no such thing. She hummed cheerfully to herself all week, quite carried away by her own enthusiasm.

'We'll buy one of their red wines, too, I think,' she decided happily as she cooked the bacon for their breakfast on Saturday morning.

Jan sighed inwardly.

'I had no idea you knew your wines so well, Grandmother. You're quite the connoisseur! At this rate,' she joked, 'you'll be bankrupt within a month.'

'Live and let live,' her grandmother quoted, adding her own homily, 'We only live once, so let it be well.'

Her eyes took on a misty hue.

'I used to visit Sans Souci quite a lot when your father did their books. At one time your parents lived on the estate, in one of the staff cottages, but that was before you were born, of course. The old man was very fond of your mother. He wanted his son, Rupert, to marry her, but my Jenny had eyes only for your father, and naturally I encouraged her. Your father was a fine man.'

She helped herself to a slice of toast from the toast rack and scraped the last of the marmalade from its jar.

'Of course, it was before . . . before that woman came on the scene and made a play for Rupert, and she up and married him before any of us could draw breath. The old man was not pleased, I can tell you! After a while we heard that she'd left Rupert with two small children and run off with a wealthy businessman, but they were both killed in a motor accident shortly afterwards.'

She paused thoughtfully.

'Raoul, I think the little boy's name was. Big for his age, too, and very energetic. He was always cycling up and down the paths. I can't remember what the girl was called.'

'Probably something French like Antoinette,' Jan suggested dryly.

'How clever you are, dear! That's it, Antoinette. Toni, they called her. Awfully nice children, they were, and away at boarding school most of the time. The boy was very polite, but you couldn't fool him for a minute. He always knew exactly what he wanted.'

I'll bet, Jan thought sourly.

There was nothing for it but to make the best of the situation, for her Grandmother's sake. They would drive out to Sans Souci and she'd tuck herself away behind the casks in the cellar while her grandmother made their purchases. She would be quite safe. From what she'd heard, the Jourdans always employed hoards of minions to do their work for them, and with any luck Raoul Jourdan would not be around.

Jan would have been disconcerted to know that he was doing no such thing. Raoul Jourdan was at that very moment in the cellar at Sans Souci, standing among the oak barrels, deep in conversation with the cellar master, Bernard Malan.

Raoul's knowledge of wine-making was considerable. He was determined to carry on the noble traditions of his forbears, a courageous and hardworking people who had emigrated three hundred years previously from the wine growing regions of France.

His knowledge of women, however, was rather more limited. He had been too wrapped up in his work to be bothered with more than the odd friendship, until last Saturday. It had only taken one meeting for him to know his own mind. And now that he'd found her, his butterfly lady, he intended to keep her.

3

Jan hurried through her morning chores so that there would be enough time to make a ham salad for their lunch. She assembled the ingredients, sliced the ham and set the table, all the while hiding her secret feeling of dread.

True to her word, her grandmother had baked a fruit tart and was busy preparing the chicken and potatoes for roasting while they were out. Mrs Burney activated the timer, content in the knowledge that by the time they returned their dinner would be ready.

The busy lunch-time traffic had eased by the time they drove out of town and turned on to the main highway stretching north. With a contented sigh Mrs Burney settled back to enjoy the outing, for it was not often she had the opportunity of reliving events of the past, and she had long wished to see once again the estate where her daughter had been so happy.

Before Jenny had married Jan's father she had worked as a personal assistant to the elderly owner, Philippe Jourdan, who had been particularly fond of the vivacious, young girl and deeply disappointed when she married Geoff Harding, the Sans Souci accountant, instead of his son. But Rupert Jourdan had been an irresponsible young man, a gambler and a womaniser, and Jenny had wanted nothing to do with him. Rupert had turned his spite on her young husband, determined to have him dismissed.

Mrs Burney shook off her sombre thoughts and looked about her with interest.

'Would you mind, dear, if I bought a loaf of that walnut bread and some cheese from the Simonsberg Cheese Factory Shop?' she added somewhat obscurely. 'It's the early bird that catches the worm, you know.'

Obligingly, Jan turned off the highway. She drew up before the long, low building which housed the cheese factory and escorted her grandmother into the shop. Hopefully, the old lady would linger over her choices, which would leave less time for their visit to Sans Souci.

'I'll take a loaf of that olive bread as well,' her grandmother decided.

'Have you seen the preserves?' Jan encouraged. 'There's prickly pear, plum and apricot. And they have the most divine cream cheeses, Grandmother. French herb, smoked salmon, garlic and parsley.'

It was half an hour later that they emerged from the shop, armed with enough treats to last them a month.

'What fun this is,' her grandmother remarked.

Jan gave her a fond glance. It took so little to please the old lady. She was more than ever determined they should enjoy the outing to Sans Souci, whatever the personal cost to herself.

Any poignant memories which surfaced would have to be firmly banished.

She turned east towards the mountains, driving through pleasant countryside where farms and vineyards stretched as far as the eye could see. At last they came to Sans Souci, the two-hundred-acre estate which nestled comfortably along the banks of the river. Row upon row of vines covered the valley and stretched up the slopes of the mountain, softly green in their budding spring finery.

'Wait until autumn,' her grandmother told her, 'when the leaves have turned rusty-gold. It's a marvellous sight.'

Marvellous or not, Jan had no intention of viewing Sans Souci in the autumn or on any other occasion, for that matter. After today she would never return to the area. Driving through an impressive entrance flanked by stone pillars, they turned into a long drive which wound between an avenue of ancient oak trees bordering a beautiful, landscaped garden. It led to a neat, paved area near the house, reserved for visitors' cars. Jan parked.

So this was Raoul Jourdan's home! It was nothing short of a carefully-restored and preserved historic manor house, and far more impressive than she had remembered. The homestead may be old, but doubtless there would be up-to-date cellar technology designed to facilitate the production of world-class wines, if her grandmother's enthusiasm could be taken as any recommendation.

Jan took her grandmother's arm and helped her negotiate the paved fore-court in front of the house.

'Isn't it marvellous?' her grand-mother declared.

A fine example of early Cape architecture, its baroque gable soared towards the sky and every facet of its multi-paned windows reflected the rosy afternoon sun. Despite herself, Jan gave a sigh of pure pleasure.

'Yes, it's amazing.'

A signboard saying **Wine Tasting**

And Sales indicated that they should follow a pathway to the left. It led to a wide, paved area of wooden tables and benches shaded by large, striped umbrellas. The pillared buildings surrounding it were impressive, whitewashed in the Cape Dutch style to match the homestead, with vines creeping over their sturdy, wooden struts.

'Ah, here is the cellar,' Mrs Burney said, obviously familiar with her surroundings. 'We'll buy our wine and then sit for a moment and enjoy the sunshine before we go, Janetta.'

'Yes, Grandmother.'

Hoping desperately that the disturbing Raoul Jourdan would be miles away by this time, Jan followed her grandmother into the gabled cellar. The interior was dimly lit by hanging lamps which gave it a prevailing air of timelessness and olde-worlde charm. Jan looked about her with real interest. It was the first time she had ever been in such a place.

Racks of bottles graced one wall

behind a large, wooden counter, and nearby, at rustic, wooden tables, sat one or two visitors who preferred to sample the wines before making their purchases. The cement floor and rough-cast walls gave the ambience of an underground cavern, somewhat dank and chilly, although it looked spotless. Jan longed to return to the sunshine and gave a little shiver, wishing she'd brought a cardigan with her.

'Yes, it's cool in here. We keep the temperature between sixteen and eighteen degrees Celsius,' a deep voice informed her.

Jan jumped.

'Oh, it's you.'

What rotten luck, meeting up with him the moment she set foot in the place! Raoul Jourdan smiled mockingly.

'Oui, mademoiselle, it is I. We meet in most unusual places, do we not?'

His intent gaze swept over her body, noting every detail of her appearance — the snug-fitting jeans sheathing her shapely form and the cotton top which revealed arms and shoulders dusted golden by the sun.

'Why are you still following me?' he demanded.

Jan gasped.

'I am not following you!'

How conceited the man was!

He ignored her look of outrage and said blandly, 'What I can't understand is this. One day you act as though I have a dead fish in my back pocket, and the next, you come all this way to pay me an unexpected visit. Forgive me if I'm confused.'

He placed a large, warm hand on her shoulder.

'I don't have snake blood in my veins, you know.'

Jan opened her mouth to reply and then closed it again, at a complete loss. Raoul seemed determined to extract an answer.

'What brings you to our maturation cellar, butterfly lady?'

'Why do people usually come here?' she snapped, furious at his arrogant assumption that she'd come to see him. 'My grandmother wishes to purchase some wine.'

In fact, if it wasn't for her grandmother she'd march right out of here this minute! Mrs Burney turned around to observe the owner of the deep voice.

'You must be the charming lady I spoke to on the telephone,' Raoul said with a smile, taking her hand. 'Welcome to Sans Souci.'

Reluctantly, Jan made the introductions.

'Grandmother, this is Mister Raoul Jourdan, of Sans Souci. My grandmother, Daffodil Burney.'

She twinkled up at Raoul, amazed to find that he was the very customer who had told her he wished to purchase flowers from Jan's Blooms.

'Is this your first visit to Sans Souci, Mrs Burney?' Raoul enquired politely.

'Oh, no, dear, I've been here many times. My daughter and her husband used to work on the estate, a long time ago.'

Raoul's eyes narrowed.

'I see. May I ask your daughter's name? I daresay it was before my time.'

'Harding. Jenny Harding. She was married to the estate accountant, Geoffrey Harding. They were Janetta's parents.'

'Janetta?'

'My granddaughter, here.'

Raoul turned his interested gaze on Jan, who stared back.

'Your name is Janetta? How charming.'

'Grandmother,' Jan intervened pointedly, 'the wine.'

'Yes, dear.'

Firmly Jan guided her grandmother towards the counter where an earnest young man with spectacles obligingly saw to Mrs Burney's wants. Jan wandered away to inspect the casks, only to find that the chalked figures on their outside were incomprehensible to her. She wandered back to the counter in time to hear Raoul tell the assistant firmly, 'There will be no charge.'

'Yes, sir.'

Jan blushed scarlet.

'We shall pay for our wine,' she insisted.

How dare he be so patronising? Anyone would think they were paupers! He smiled charmingly.

'It is my gift to your grandmother, because she has very kindly agreed to have tea with me.'

Jan looked from him to her grandmother, her mouth open.

'Tea?'

'You don't mind, Jan?'

There was a trace of anxiety in her grandmother's eyes.

'Mister Jourdan has very kindly offered to show us around the manor house afterwards, and I have always longed to see the interior. I may not have another opportunity. We must make hay while the sun shines.'

Jan swallowed. The afternoon was not turning out at all how she had planned. Then she remembered her earlier resolve that her grandmother should enjoy the outing, and summoned a bright smile.

'How kind of Mister Jourdan, Grandmother. You will enjoy that.'

With a self-satisfied smile, Raoul took her grandmother's arm.

'Please, call me Raoul.'

Controlling her rising frustration, Jan followed them out into the sunshine. It appeared that Mister Jourdan was a man who always expected to have his own way. Well, she had news for him! Mindful of Mrs Burney's difficulty in walking long distances, Raoul curtailed his stride, escorting them slowly up the path to the main entrance of the house.

Jan looked around the vast hall and was intrigued to see that the original hand-hewn yellowwood floors and ceilings, darkened by time to a rich honey colour, were still in place. Vast doors opened from the hall, at one end of which a massive staircase curved to the gallery above. A dumpy, middle-aged woman in a black dress appeared from the nether regions of the house, her dark hair scraped back severely and her pallid, unremarkable features completely devoid of expression.

'Ah, Mrs Blignaut, this is Mrs Burney and Miss Janetta Harding, come to take tea with me. May we have it in the small sitting-room?'

'Certainly, sir.'

To Jan's surprise the housekeeper darted them a look of intense dislike before offering, 'Would the ladies like to tidy themselves first, sir?'

Wordlessly she led Jan and her grandmother to a cloakroom beneath the massive, curving staircase, and just as silently disappeared.

'Unfriendly woman,' Jan remarked as she ran a brush through her hair.

'She's positively poison,' her grandmother agreed. 'I remember her well. She was a young girl, one of the housemaids, in fact, when your parents worked here. I never liked her. She was Marta Smit in those days, and she was always making trouble.'

'Marta Smit,' Jan mused. 'The

name's familiar.'

Raoul was waiting for them in the hall.

'This way,' he invited, ushering them into a cosy sitting-room.

Despite the sunshine which poured in through the tall, timbered windows, there was a small log fire crackling in the fireplace.

'A house this size can be chilly,' Raoul explained, 'so we light our fires until the end of spring.'

He seated them in comfortable armchairs and shooed a matronly tabby cat off the brocade sofa before lowering his great frame on to it. Jan looked about her, noting with pleasure the mixture of period pieces and modern, comfortable seating. Strategically-placed lamp tables held lamps with the same rosy shades which were echoed in the thick wool carpet and the velvet curtains. The walls were washed with a pale, silvery green, and one or two watercolours graced them, all depicting floral themes, she observed with satisfaction. It was a pleasant, lived-in room. If she were the mistress of the house, she'd adopt this room as her own, and sit here in the afternoons while the children did their homework. All that was missing was a decent floral arrangement — pink roses, she decided, with touches of gold and one or two sprays of grey-green.

Raoul watched the pleasure on her face and smiled faintly. His butterfly lady was impressed, as well she should be. He was immensely proud of his heritage and it delighted him to be able to share its beauties.

Mrs Blignaut carried in a large tray and placed it on the sofa table, all the while darting dark glances at them from beneath her brows.

'Shall I pour the tea?' Jan offered.

'Please.'

There were tiny sandwiches, a fruit cake and light-as-air fairy cakes on the dainty china plates. Whatever her faults, Raoul's housekeeper knew how to bake,

Jan reflected, noting her grandmother's contented sigh as she handed her a cup of tea. The old lady's pleasure was worth every moment of her own private discomfort.

Raoul cleared his throat.

'What do you think of Sans Souci, butterfly lady?'

Before Jan could reply, her grandmother looked at him in puzzlement.

'Why do you call her that?'

Raoul's mouth twitched as his gaze rested on Jan's bright head of hair.

'It's a long story, Mrs Burney, but to cut it short, your granddaughter reminds me of a Painted Lady.'

The old lady looked taken aback.

'A painted lady?'

'Yes. It's a particularly colourful butterfly. I especially enjoy the Yellow Pansy variety — bright, golden things which frequently sport with other butterflies.'

'Oh, I see. How extraordinary,' she murmured.

Jan hoped her heightened colour

wasn't too noticeable. He was referring to her falling all over him in that daisy field, of course. Honestly, the man was so stupid!

Tired out from all the excitement, Mrs Burney dozed off in the car on the way home, which gave Jan the opportunity of a few quiet moments' reflection. Never in her life had she come across so many treasured possessions under one roof. The house had beautifully-proportioned rooms filled with well cared for yellowwood furniture made in the Cape, not to mention the ornate antique French pieces. Priceless carpets covered the floors and there were innumerable cabinets filled with valuable porcelain. It boggled the mind!

By the time Raoul had finished showing them around, both she and her grandmother had been ecstatic. Then he'd spoiled it by pointing out blandly that all Sans Souci lacked were suitable floral arrangements. Jan agreed.

'Why don't you commission Janetta?' her grandmother had suggested, adding proudly, 'My granddaughter is very professional, you know. She'll do a good job.'

'Oh, I know that. The truth is I've already asked her, Mrs Burney, but she has refused to help me. I suppose I shall have to find someone else.'

'Refused?'

Her grandmother had turned disbelieving blue eyes upon her.

'Is that true, Janetta? You have refused to help Raoul with his flowers?'

'That is correct, Grandmother,' she'd said firmly, shooting Raoul a furious look.

It had been an interesting day, Jan reflected as she drove through the streets of Stellenbosch, but one she was unlikely ever to repeat. As for Raoul Jourdan, he was the most dangerous man she'd ever laid eyes on and she would do well to avoid him in future.

Jan and her grandmother spent a pleasant evening, dining like queens. The Sans Souci wine, Jan was forced to admit, was everything her grandmother had promised. She then took herself to bed after watching her favourite television programme, content in the knowledge that the whole Sans Souci episode could now be relegated to the past. As for the disturbing Mister Jourdan, she would never see hide nor hair of him again.

At two o'clock the following morning Jan awoke in a cold sweat. She sat bolt upright in bed and stared into the darkness. It had been a particularly nasty dream.

She'd been playing in the garden at Sans Souci while her father worked in the estate office behind the homestead. It was a cold, blustery day and she'd been about to go inside to find him when she overheard the housemaid telling the gardener that her father was in deep, deep trouble. Her eight-year-old eyes had filled with tears. She'd rushed up to them and demanded to know why.

'He's a bad one, your father,' the housemaid had informed her with malicious satisfaction. 'He stole all Mister Philippe's money and put it on the horses, now he's lost it all, and can't pay it back. Mister Rupert says he'll have to leave Sans Souci. Mister Rupert says he'll go to prison. You'll all go to prison!'

The scene came rushing back with startling clarity, only it hadn't simply been a dream, it had really happened. Jan realised that she had buried the childhood memory deep in her subconscious because of the painful events which had followed, and now the visit to Sans Souci had stirred it up again. She gasped aloud as a further piece of the puzzle fell into place.

The spiteful housemaid had been none other than Marta Smit, now Blignaut.

'Awful woman!' Jan breathed.

There was no way she could go back to sleep without a hot drink so she put on her dressing-gown and slippers and padded to the kitchen. While she waited, Jan's thoughts reverted to the time of her father's death. Because she had never understood the circumstances surrounding the tragic event, she had been unable to gain real closure and move on with her life. She'd been left with the dread that she would one day marry a man who would go away from her, as her father had done. The hurt and anger of it had been devastating. As for his alleged crime, she had conveniently forgotten about it, unable to face the shame.

The nagging thought persisted that he might have done something wrong, after all. Yet how could this be? He had been the most honourable man she'd ever known. She sighed uncertainly. As Sans Souci's accountant, her father would have known how to gain access to estate money. What if he had defrauded the Jourdans, when all this time she had imagined them to have been the guilty ones!

What she'd heard in the garden that day had been a shock to the small, lonely girl who had idolised her father, especially since her mother had died the previous year after a long, harrowing illness. She remembered clearly the look on her father's face as he'd taken her home that day. She remembered how he had sat on the sofa and put his head in his hands and cried, and then she'd been sent to her grandmother's, and then had come the day she'd been told he was dead.

It was time, she decided, to uncover the truth. It was only when she knew the true facts she could face up to them. If her father had truly been guilty, then she would undertake to pay back to the estate every penny he owed, even if it took a lifetime! Despite her earlier reluctance, she would be going back to Sans Souci, after all!

4

On Sunday mornings Jan usually took her grandmother a breakfast tray in bed, after which they dressed and went to church for the morning service. This morning, however, Mrs Burney announced unexpectedly that she would stay in bed until lunchtime as she was a little tired.

'You do that, Grandmother. I'll see to lunch when I return from church, so you're not to bother about it.'

The old lady sank back on to her pillows and closed her eyes.

'Thank you, dear.'

Jan hurried through her chores and went to tidy herself. It wasn't like her grandmother to miss church, but she'd obviously been overdoing things a little. Perhaps the excitement of her visit to Sans Souci had been too much for her. The memories it evoked would certainly have been poignant. At the thought of Sans Souci, Jan's own emotions swirled like washing in a tub. It would be difficult, but she must go through with her decision. It was imperative to gain the information she sought, even if she had to go through the estate records herself.

The vicar's sermon, appropriately enough, was about discovering the truth, and as a result, Jan left the church more than ever determined to embark on her quest. She walked from the church to the adjacent carpark, deep in thought.

'Why so glum, butterfly lady?' Raoul's gravelly voice cut into her thoughts. 'It's far too nice a morning to mooch around in carparks looking like a duck in a desert.'

Jan jumped.

'I am not mooching! And I wish you wouldn't sneak up on me like that. It's unsettling.'

'You have such a short fuse,' Raoul observed calmly.

'And you are the most annoying man I have ever met.'

She shoved her car key forcefully into the lock.

'While we're trading insults, let me tell you what I think! I think you . . . '

Raoul stopped her in full flow by the only method he could think of. He planted a firm kiss on her surprised mouth. Jan blinked.

'You . . . you . . . '

'You were saying?' he prompted.

She took a deep breath in order to steady herself.

'I was going to say that I think you're so conceited you think the sun comes up in order to hear you crow.'

Raoul gave a shout of laughter.

'Fair comment.'

He removed her car key and slipped it into his pocket.

'I'm taking you over the road for a cup of coffee.'

'But I don't want one,' Jan felt compelled to argue.

She wasn't going to be bossed

around by some macho man with a huge ego. Before she could draw breath, however, he had shepherded her into the small café opposite the carpark.

'A nice cup of tea,' he coaxed, 'and a pastry?'

Rather ungraciously Jan agreed.

'Well, all right, then, as it seems I have no choice.'

Once seated she looked him straight in the eye.

'What do you want? Why are you in Stellenbosch? I've never seen you at our church before.'

Without hesitation he told her the truth.

'I was hoping for a glimpse of you.'

Jan was speechless. Why would he want to see her? They couldn't say one civil word to each other.

Before she could formulate any further questions, he explained smoothly.

'I'm on my way to visit my sister, Antoinette. I had to pass through Stellenbosch so I stopped off at the church in the hope that you'd be there.'

Jan digested this in silence. He was a most confusing man. Anyone would think he actually liked her! In the small shop, she sipped her tea and remembered her resolve of the night before.

'I've changed my mind about your flowers by the way,' she blurted. 'I'll do them.'

Raoul eyed her inscrutably over the rim of his cup.

'Oh?'

'Now that I've actually seen Sans Souci,' Jan rushed on, 'I can see what you mean. You would need at least six large arrangements for the reception rooms, and some small posies for the bedrooms. I would like to see all the rooms again before I give you a quotation for the work.'

His mouth twitched.

'To what do we owe this sudden change of heart?'

Jan cast about in her mind for something to say. She could hardly inform him that she intended to go to Sans Souci in order to investigate her father's supposedly unsavoury past, could she?

'I need the business,' she said, a little too quickly.

'I see.'

Undeceived, Raoul concealed his satisfaction behind a grave face.

'In that case, we had better conclude the deal as quickly as possible, had we not? When would you like to visit Sans Souci?'

Mentally reviewing her week, Jan decided that Tuesday would be a good day. She would drive out to Raoul's home and work there for the rest of the week. It would mean asking Clarc to work a few extra shifts, but her loyal employee would be glad to earn a little extra money.

'Tuesday. It should take me about four days to complete the task,' she explained, exaggerating slightly.

Normally she worked quicker than that, but the extra time spent at the estate would be useful.

'Then you will be accommodated at Sans Souci for the duration.'

'Oh, that's not necessary. I could easily drive out every day. I can't leave Grandmother.'

'Your grandmother is quite capable of looking after herself for a few days, Janetta. She would be the first to say that. Besides, you need uninterrupted time in order to remain focused. I do not want any half measures.'

'I always produce work of a high standard!' she retorted.

'I am pleased to hear it.'

Raoul drained his tea cup and added silkily, 'Furthermore, since your business is struggling, you would not wish to incur the extra expense of daily travel.'

Jan opened her mouth to protest that her business had never been healthier, but thought better of it. He was right. Uninterrupted time is what she needed. She had the estate books to peruse with a fine tooth comb.

'That's settled then,' she told him firmly. 'Goodbye, Raoul. I'll see you on Tuesday.'

Raoul escorted her to the car and stared thoughtfully as she drove away. His butterfly lady was up to something, and he would make it his business to find out what it was!

On Monday, Jan reassessed her stock and found it to be completely inadequate for what she had in mind for Sans Souci. Leaving Clare in charge of the shop, she drove to various wholesalers in Cape Town and bought more supplies, ferreting out the finest, most exquisite material she could lay her hands on. She was determined not to consider the cost. Raoul Jourdan was obviously a man of means, and he had told her to deliver only the best, so she would. And what a pleasure that would be!

On Tuesday morning, Jan parked her car in the narrow yard behind the shop. She gave Clare a few last-minute instructions before reversing her little black van, loaded with numerous large, flat boxes, out into the street. Ten minutes later she arrived at the cottage in order to collect the small suitcase she had packed the previous evening. Mrs Burney heard the van's arrival and hurriedly switched on the kettle.

'You'll have a cup of coffee before you go, Janetta,' she said firmly, 'and one of my apple scones.'

'All right, Grandmother.' Jan grinned. 'I daresay I need to keep up my strength for all that creativity.'

The statement was not wholly true, for there was nothing she liked better than arranging flowers. The activity energised her incredibly.

Her grandmother set a steaming mug of coffee before her.

'See that you do a good job, then, dear.'

'Oh, I will. In fact, I can't wait to start.'

Hastily, Jan took a sip of coffee, shocked at her thoughts. What she'd really meant was she couldn't wait to see Raoul Jourdan again. The strange thing was that although she disliked him intensely, he fascinated her out of her mind. He attracted her, no doubt about it, but was that warmth of personality and smooth charm to be trusted?

Mrs Burney lowered herself stiffly into a chair, helped herself to a scone and observed forthrightly, 'Raoul Jourdan is in love with you, Janetta.'

'That's ridiculous! We've only just met. He thinks I'm a joke.'

'Nonsense.' She sighed. 'You're a tad short with him. Do try to like him a little, will you? He would make a fine husband, and I'm not getting any younger, remember? I should like to see you settled.'

'Yes, Grandmother,' Jan agreed meekly, hiding her annoyance.

It was no use arguing with the old dear. Her grandmother could be as determined as she liked, it would not alter the fact that she would never marry a Jourdan. If the truth be told, she was still convinced that the Jourdan family had ruined her father's life. What's more, it was not long now and she would be able to prove it!

An hour later, Jan arrived at Sans Souci. She negotiated the long drive in her little van and eventually drew up behind the house where the staff garages were situated. One of the estate workers showed her where to park, obviously having been told to watch for her arrival. He carried her suitcase to the side entrance which was reserved for staff, and deposited it on the floor just inside the door before disappearing once more.

So she was to be treated like any other employee, Jan thought wryly. She started when Mrs Blignaut appeared silently behind her.

'Come this way, please, Miss Harding.'

'Oh! Good morning, Mrs Blignaut.'

'You will use the staff entrance at all times, and refer to me should you need anything,' the woman told her officiously. 'I will not have the other servants distracted from their tasks.'

'I am not a servant,' Jan pointed out sweetly. 'I have been professionally commissioned by Raoul Jourdan to provide decorations for his home. Be good enough to show me to my room, please.'

The housekeeper's eyes narrowed in spite.

'I was about to do that, miss, and you will kindly remember that Mister Raoul does not like visitors to roam about at will. You are to inform me of your whereabouts at all times. I must know exactly where you will be working, on which day. Is that clear?'

'Oh, you need not concern yourself with my comings and goings, Mrs Blignaut,' Jan replied airily, determined not to be browbeaten by the frightful woman. 'I am sure you have enough to do without bothering about me all the time. I shall only be here for a few days, after all. Do I take my meals with the rest of the staff?'

'Certainly. Come this way.'

With a sour face, Mrs Blignaut preceded her down the passage. Jan picked up her suitcase with a satisfied smile. When she wasn't busy arranging flowers, she would be snooping about the offices or picking the brains of the servants, so it suited her just fine to eat with them. Besides, the less she saw of Raoul Jourdan during the next few days, the better for her peace of mind.

'You will work here, in the flower room,' Mrs Blignaut informed her, flinging open a door.

The room, at the rear of the house, contained a large table, a sink and some shelving on which lay various items of floristry equipment and one or two gardening and floral art books. On later examination, Jan found that they had belonged to a Jeanette Jourdan, who-ever she was.

Mrs Blignaut's small black eyes swept the room.

'Your boxes will be carried in by one of the gardeners, and you will tidy up any mess you make before you leave,' Jan was informed shortly.

She fully expected to be given a bedroom in the servants' quarters and was pleasantly surprised when Mrs Blignaut showed her to a large, airy upstairs room with a magnificent view of the mountains. On Raoul's instructions, perhaps? Briskly she was informed about the mealtimes.

'Breakfast is at seven o'clock, lunch at one and dinner in the evening. You will be expected to be on time, Miss Harding. A maid will bring you morning and afternoon tea.'

Clearly irritated at the inconvenience of having to deal with her, Mrs Blignaut sailed off to another part of the house.

'I have another quote for Grandmother,' Jan muttered to herself as she unpacked her few belongings — everyone has a purpose in life, if only to serve as a bad example. How on earth such an unpleasant person had managed to keep her job for so long was a mystery. Raoul obviously found her satisfactory. Some men couldn't see what was going on under their very noses!

Hastily Jan ran a brush through her hair, re-applied her lipstick and returned to the flower room. She discovered that her boxes had been stacked neatly against the wall, together with her basket of tools and her work apron. Before she could start, however, she needed to take another look at all those rooms.

Slowly Jan toured the house, jotting down notes on her pad as she re-acquainted herself with its beauties. Her eyes shone and her heart raced as she contemplated in her mind's eye the various style of arrangement which would suit each room. Never had she had such an exciting commission! She would begin with a large, eye-catching arrangement for the copper bowl in the entrance hall.

It was already lunchtime by the time she returned to the small room with her notes. She went to wash her hands in the cloakroom beneath the stairs which she and her grandmother had used on their first visit, and re-emerged to look about her uncertainly. The housekeeper had not told her where to find the staff dining-room. A uniformed housemaid appeared at her elbow.

'Miss Harding?'

Jan smiled.

'Yes.'

'I am Magda. Mrs Blignaut said you are to eat with us, miss.'

There was a note of disapproval in her tones.

'Lead the way, then, Magda.'

Around the large table in the staff dining-room sat an assortment of people who all fell silent as Jan entered. Clearly they were uncomfortable at having her eat with them. Jan smiled in a friendly fashion, took the seat Magda indicated and began a light-hearted conversation with the woman beside her. Within minutes the atmosphere had relaxed.

'Where is Mrs Blignaut?' Jan enquired

of Magda, seated on the other side of her.

'She eats in her own apartment, miss. A good thing, too. She's so sour, she'd curdle our cream.'

A sentiment with which Jan heartily agreed, but it wasn't her place to say so. She decided there was no time like the present to begin probing.

'I daresay Mrs Blignaut has worked here for a long time.'

'Oh, yes, miss, a very long time.'

'Are there any members of staff who have been here longer?'

Magda gave the matter some thought.

'Well, there's Jacob, the head gardener, and there's old Mister Crewe, who works in the estate office. He was here when old Monsieur Philippe, Mister Raoul's grandfather, was alive.'

Jan filed these names away for future reference. They made two very good places to start.

After lunch she returned to the flower room and immediately became lost in her glorious world of blooms. When she had finished, she carried the copper bowl back into the hall, placed it carefully on the oak table and stood back to admire the artful display which echoed the colours of the expensive Persian rugs strewn across the polished floor.

'Very nice,' Raoul approved, entering through the massive front door.

Jan spun around. She thanked him sedately, trying to subdue her rocketing pulses. What was it about the man that threw her so off kilter? He came into the hall, placed his briefcase on the floor and kissed her. It was a satisfying kiss, the memory of which Jan decided to tuck away in one corner of her mind so that she could take it out and examine it when she felt more able. Right now she had great difficulty in keeping her thoughts straight.

'I am sorry I was not here when you arrived,' he apologised with a smile. 'I have only just returned from a wine growers' meeting in Cape Town. I trust you enjoyed your lunch.'

'Oh, yes, thank you. We had chicken casserole, apple tart and cream, and it was all beautifully cooked and very tasty.'

'We? You dined with Mrs Blignaut?'

'No. I dined with the rest of the servants.'

He gave her a long look.

'I see. On whose instructions?'

'Your housekeeper's.'

'An unfortunate error. Please accept my apologies. You will dine with me in future,' he informed her in a bland voice, but Jan noticed that his eyes were coldly angry.

Raoul retrieved his briefcase and made for the study.

'I won't keep you from your work.'

Jan returned to the flower room and began to plan her next arrangement, a display on a pedestal for one corner of the drawing-room. It would have to be as elegant as the furnishings, and she needed to concentrate fully. Later on she would have time to think about the proposed visit to old Mister Crewe, and she'd also think about the meaning of that kiss from Raoul.

At six-thirty, Jan went upstairs to her bedroom to change out of her black trousers. If she was expected to dine with Raoul, she had better look presentable. Fortunately she had packed a long, velvet skirt. It was the colour of sapphires and had a matching silk blouse with pin tucks on the bodice and lace at the cuffs. The colour gave added depth to her eyes and acted as a foil for her pale, shining hair.

She took a shower, re-did her make-up and dressed with practised speed, slipping her feet into a pair of high-heeled sandals before checking to see that her hair was perfect. She had coiled it into a smooth chignon, leaving artful wisps about her temples.

Raoul's breath caught as he watched her descend the wide staircase. His butterfly looked both elegant and sophisticated tonight, a fitting mistress for the other love of his life, Sans Souci.

From the moment he'd laid eyes on Jan Harding, the decision had been made. This was the woman he'd been waiting for.

He smiled as Jan reached the last step, and took her by the arm.

'A drink before dinner, I think.'

He ushered her into the drawing-room she'd vacated less than an hour ago, when she'd carefully placed an exquisite arrangement on the mahogany pedestal in the corner. Raoul seated her on a charming Victorian love-seat and went to the cabinet to dispense the drinks. His gaze was caught by the arrangement on the pedestal and he paused for a moment in sheer disbelief.

'Is that your work?' he asked with a mixture of amusement and consternation.

Good grief, even he could tell it looked like a dog's breakfast! In fact, a drunken chimpanzee with a broken arm could have done better.

'Yes.'

Jan turned to view the arrangement

with a smile. The smile froze. Her eyes widened in horrified disbelief. Instead of the beauty she'd left there, it was now nothing but a mess! While she'd been upstairs, someone had broken the twigs, bent the flower heads and disarranged the colours. Her superb artistry was no longer even recognisable.

5

Jan turned appalled eyes on Raoul's face, speechless at what had happened. Eventually, she was able to say what she felt.

'That certainly is not my work!' she gasped.

'Thank goodness for that. I was having second thoughts about having hired you.'

His eyes gleamed with amusement.

'It's no laughing matter,' Jan snapped. 'Someone has deliberately spoiled my work. I left a charming arrangement in here before I went upstairs, and now I find this! Why would anybody do a thing like that?'

'More to the point,' he said quietly, 'who?'

Jan took a deep breath.

'It must be some kind of a sick joke.'

'Perhaps,' he said and his eyes

narrowed. 'I shall make enquiries. In the meantime, if you are quite finished with your drink, we'll go in to dinner.'

The meal could have been sawdust for all the notice Jan took of it. Magda served them a delicious seafood starter followed by prime fillet steak with wild mushrooms. Even the tangy lemon sorbet made no impression. She toyed with it abstractedly while Raoul enjoyed the cheese board, his appetite apparently unimpaired.

Who could possibly wish to harm her professional reputation? Who could hate her that much?

Magda served their coffee in the small sitting-room, departing with a sunny smile after enquiring if they needed anything further. At least one of Raoul's staff was both pleasant and polite, Jan reflected. The girl had seemed willing to talk, too. In the morning she would seek Magda out and begin her own investigations. Despite her doubts, a part of her still could not believe that her father was a thief. She intended to prove his innocence if it was the last thing she did.

But Magda had been given the day off. Jan made discreet enquiries in the morning and discovered that Susanne, another of the servants, would be bringing her tea. She occupied herself re-doing the ruined arrangement for the drawing-room and set about selecting material for a posy in a basket. For once her work gave her no pleasure. She was impatient to be about her real business, that of clearing her father's name.

At eleven o'clock promptly, Susanne knocked and entered with a tray.

'Your tea, miss,' she said and Jan thanked her and replied with a smile, 'You must be Susanne.'

'Yes, miss.'

'Perhaps you can help me. Which of the servants was on duty in the house last night?'

'Only Magda and I, miss. Magda served Master Raoul's dinner while I cleaned up in the kitchen. I helped with the cooking, too, because the cook, Thomas, went home early. His wife is ill.'

'And Mrs Blignaut?'

'Mrs Blignaut finishes her duties at six-thirty each day, miss. She goes up to her flat and we serve her dinner there at six-forty five.'

And where was Mrs Blignaut between six-thirty and six forty-five, Jan wondered. Paying a covert visit to the drawing-room, perhaps?

'I see. Thank you,' she said to Susanne.

'Is there anything wrong, miss?'

Jan smiled again.

'No. Tell me, when would be the best time to visit Mister Crew or Jacob, the head gardener?'

'Jacob is not here on a Wednesday but old Mister Crew should be in the office until one o'clock,' the maid informed her obligingly. 'He only works mornings.'

Jan thanked her, put the finishing touch to her arrangement and sat down to drink her tea while she pondered her next move. It was already almost eleven-thirty. If she wished to see Mister Crewe, she had better go immediately. She tidied away the debris from her morning's work, placing it in the bin provided, and stepped out of the flower room, and immediately came face to face with Mrs Blignaut.

'Susanne tells me you wish to know about the servants' off duties,' the housekeeper accused her, bridling with annoyance. 'Kindly confine yourself to your own business, Miss Harding.'

'It is my business, Mrs Blignaut, when one of your staff sees fit to interfere with my work,' Jan explained sweetly.

The other woman eyed her sharply.

'Interfere? What are you talking about?'

'Someone deliberately wrecked one of my arrangements last night between six-thirty and seven o'clock, in the drawing-room.'

There was a slight pause.

'Yes, so Mister Raoul said.'

Mrs Blignaut's dark eyes glowed with some secret emotion.

'I told him I knew nothing about it,' she said then added with a slight sneer, 'I said it is my belief you produced something distinctly inferior and decided to say it had been sabotaged.'

Speechless at this further evidence of the woman's malice, Jan blinked.

'You are mistaken,' she declared when she'd found her voice. 'It was sabotaged, and, believe me, I shall find out who it was!'

With her head in the air, she turned and walked on down the passage.

'Where are you going?' Mrs Blignaut demanded.

'To the cloakroom,' Jan retorted, and kept on walking.

She did indeed visit the cloakroom, if only to calm herself before slipping out of one of the side doors into the garden. She skirted the bushes beside the kitchen, taking care not to be seen, and found the path to the offices. The receptionist was chattily indiscreet.

'Mister Crew? Down the passage, second door on the left. Are you a relative? The old dear doesn't get many visitors these days, which is a pity.'

'No, I'm . . . er . . . the daughter of a friend,' Jan improvised.

Well, her parents would have known him when they'd worked here, wouldn't they?

'Oh, well, it's a good thing you're visiting then. He doesn't have enough to do now that our books are done by a firm in Stellenbosch. The old dear wasn't up to it any more,' she explained, 'and Mister Raoul didn't want to make him redundant so he kept him on.'

In which case, Jan thought, Mister Crewe would not mind sparing her half an hour of his time. Unfortunately, it looked as though she wouldn't be able to gain access to any records if they were kept in Stellenbosch, but she'd pick his brains instead. Taking a deep breath, she knocked on the door, still having no clear idea of what she wished to say to the man.

The thin, elderly gentleman sitting at the mahogany desk put aside the book he was reading and glanced up in surprise. It wasn't every day he was favoured with a visit from an attractive young lady. It was a welcome sight which immediately livened up his day.

'Good morning,' he beamed, rising to shake Jan's hand. 'Take a seat, take a seat. What can I do for you, my dear young lady?'

He ushered her to a plush red armchair and seated her, his manner charmingly old-fashioned. He seated himself opposite her in the other chair and surveyed her with interest. Jan liked him immediately.

'Mister Crewe?'

'Harvey Crewe, at your service. How can I help you, my dear?'

'Mister Crewe, I'm on a little jaunt down memory lane,' Jan began. 'My parents used to live on the Sans Souci estate and I'm after any information you can give me. They are both deceased, and I understand that you have been here for many years, so I thought you may remember them.'

Harvey Crewe eyed her sympathetically.

'Both gone, you say? How unfortunate. Who are your parents, my dear?'

'My name is Jan Harding. I'm the daughter of Geoffrey and Jenny Harding. My father used to be the accountant at Sans Souci.'

'Geoff Harding?'

The old man looked astounded.

'Of course I knew Geoff. I took his job here after he'd . . . er . . . gone. Sad business.'

'Yes. Did you know my father well?'

'I worked on the neighbouring estate, La Mont, and when the vacancy arose here, I applied for it. Geoff and I, though not exactly contemporaries, were fairly close, you know. He used to confide in me sometimes. He was a good man, my dear, as you no doubt know. Would you like a cup of tea?'

Thinking it would prolong the interview, Jan accepted. She watched as Mister Crewe switched on the kettle in one corner of the room and set about finding the teabags.

'Did you know my mother?' Jan coaxed.

'Jenny? Yes. She was the daughter of my late wife's friend, Daffodil Burney. I've rather lost touch with dear Daffodil. Is she still living?'

'Oh, yes. She and I share a cottage in Stellenbosch. I am sure she would love to hear from you, Mister Crewe.'

'She would? How kind.'

He passed Jan a cup and resumed his seat.

'Awfully cut up, Geoff was, when Jenny died. You must have been quite young then.'

'Yes. I was almost eight years old.'

Without complaint, Jan took a sip of the milkless tea. Mister Crewe had forgotten to offer the sugar, too, but she didn't remind him. His blue eyes were misty as he reminisced about the past, and she allowed him to ramble on. She was just wondering how to introduce the subject of her fathers' financial affairs, when he said out of the blue, 'Geoff was as honest as the day is long. Not like that Rupert Jourdan.'

'The son of Philippe Jourdan? He was dishonest?'

'My dear, did you not hear about all the fuss? No, I suppose you would have been too young. It was just before your father died.'

'What happened?'

'Well, Rupert rather thought he might marry your mother, but she had eyes for Geoff Harding alone. Handsome young man, he was, and very good at his job. From then on Rupert had it in for Geoff, and tried repeatedly to discredit him with the old man so that he would be dismissed. Then came the matter of the money which went missing.'

'Will you tell me about it, please?'

Mister Crewe cleared his throat.

'A substantial sum of estate money was stolen, I believe. Rupert Jourdan accused Geoff, who swore he was innocent. Eventually it was discovered that it was Rupert himself who had taken the money and gambled it away, hoping to incriminate Geoff. The old man was livid, I can tell you. Cut Rupert out of his will, so that on his death everything went to young Raoul, which is just as well, for Rupert died within the year. Killed in that fast car of his.'

'So my father's name was cleared then?'

'Oh, yes, no doubt about that at all.'

A great wave of relief washed over Jan, followed by anger that she had been lied to as a child, with the result that she'd endured many years of secret misery, and all for nothing.

'What month of the year did this happen?' she persisted.

The old man paused to think.

'It was a month or two after we had

harvested the grapes. March of that year, I believe.'

Jan stared at him in disbelief. March — that was two months before her father's death. He'd died just after her eighth birthday in May. She stood up, too upset to hear any more.

'Thank you, Mister Crewe, you've been most helpful.'

'Do come and see me again, my dear.'

'Yes. Yes, perhaps I shall. Goodbye, Mister Crewe.'

As fast as she could, Jan got herself out of the office and hurried back to the house, her thoughts in total disarray. Taking deep gulps of air, she calmed herself enough to look tolerably composed as she went up to her room to tidy herself for lunch.

Glancing in the mirror, Jan saw nothing of the sudden pallor in her cheeks or the confusion in her eyes. All she could think of was that her father had not taken his life as a result of Jourdan treachery after all, because the business about the missing money had happened two months before! Everything she had always believed about the owners of Sans Souci, then, had been incorrect. But if her father's employers had not been responsible for his death, who had? And why had she expressly been told by Marta Smit, now Marta Blignaut, that her father was in disgrace and would have to leave Sans Souci?

Nothing made sense. The only bright spot in the whole sorry mess was the fact that she would not have to repay any money to the estate after all. Abstractedly Jan dug into her make-up purse, found a lipstick and applied it. Assuming a calm expression, she went down to the dining-room for lunch.

Raoul's gaze followed the fluttering of her pretty hands as Jan unfolded her table napkin. He intended before long to place on one of those hands an antique ring which had been in his family for generations. He reminded himself that he must be patient a little longer. His butterfly was not a woman to be hurried. He observed her through half-closed eyes as she spooned her soup. Jan did not seem quite herself today.

'How is the work progressing?' he asked.

He had not seen her at breakfast, having left earlier for the vineyards, and was finding that being away from her for any length of time left him feeling restless. He would need to take himself firmly in hand. Their relationship hadn't even reached first base, and he was acting like a besotted husband. He allowed himself a smile. If this was love, he had it badly!

'Oh, er, fine,' Jan replied, injecting enthusiasm into her voice. 'I intend to make up a few smaller posies this afternoon, for the bedrooms, you know.'

'Good.'

Raoul buttered a roll and broached the subject which had been on his mind all morning.

'I spoke to Mrs Blignaut about that spoiled flower arrangement. She knew nothing about it.'

'I know. I spoke to her, too.'

He kept his voice casual.

'You did? Then you'll know her opinion on the matter.'

'Indeed,' Jan said sweetly. 'She implied that I'm hopeless at my job.'

'I wish you to know that I do not agree. It is my belief that one of the servants knocked the pedestal over by mistake and was afraid to own up.'

Jan took a deep breath. At least Raoul believed in her abilities! However, she did not for one moment believe it had all been an accident. She smiled.

'Thank you. Anyway, the rest of my work will speak for itself.'

'It already has.'

As soon as she could, Jan excused herself and returned to the flower room where she worked intensely for the rest of the day, amazed to find that Raoul's vote of confidence had made all the difference to her motivation. She found herself thinking about him more and more as the afternoon wore on, and hoping that her work would please him. It was both a pleasure and an honour to be able to add some beauty to his wonderful home.

One thing was becoming obvious, she reflected as she wielded her wire clippers with practised ease. The Jourdan family, apart from Rupert, that is, was not as black as she had insisted on painting it. The only person at all who still appeared to be suspect was Marta Blignaut. If she wanted to discover more about the past, she would have to get the woman to talk, an undoubtedly impossible task!

Just after six-thirty, Jan carried a small arrangement up to the house-keeper's apartment on the top floor and tapped on the door. Mrs Blignaut's face expressed annoyance when she saw who it was.

'What do you want?'

'I thought you might like some flowers for your living-room, Mrs Blignaut,' Jan told her, summoning a smile. 'May I come in?'

After a moment's hesitation, the housekeeper stood aside rather ungraciously.

'You may put it down over there,' she told Jan, indicating a small table in the hall. 'Run along now, Miss Harding. I am expecting my dinner to be sent up at any moment.'

Jan was not to be dismissed that easily.

'Yes, well, while I'm here, perhaps you will be good enough to answer a few questions.'

'Questions?'

Mrs Blignaut's black eyes narrowed suspiciously.

'What sort of questions?'

Jan took a deep breath and plunged in.

'When I was almost eight years old, I came to Sans Souci with my father one day. You were Marta Smit then, one of the housemaids. You were in the garden, speaking to the gardener, and I distinctly remember you informing me that my father was responsible for the theft of a large sum of money from the Sans Souci estate. You also said that he would be dismissed. Why did you say that, when it wasn't true?'

Marta Blignaut stared at her expressionlessly.

'Why?' Jan insisted. 'It was a lie, wasn't it?'

The housekeeper's face hardened into a frightening mask of hate.

'Yes, it was a lie. A damned good lie, too, I thought, and it served Geoff Harding right! All the servants believed me. They discussed it for days,' she ended in satisfaction.

Anger rose in Jan's throat.

'My father was an honourable man. What had he ever done to you, to deserve such treatment?'

'It wasn't what he'd done, you stupid girl!' Mrs Blignaut spat out. 'It's what he hadn't done! He didn't make me his wife, when he ought to have done, see? I could have given him so much more than she could, but he preferred that hoity-toity daughter of

Daffodil Burney's, with her ladylike airs and her posh education. He didn't even know I existed!'

Her lips twisted into an ugly sneer.

'He married her, and for eight long years he didn't even give me the time of day. So I fixed him, didn't I? I told them all he'd taken the money, when I knew all along it was Rupert Jourdan. He told me so himself, when he'd had too much to drink. Your father squirmed for days, I can tell you.'

'You're despicable.'

Mrs Blignaut smiled, her mouth split into a triumphant smirk.

'And you're just like her, prancing about as though you own the place. Well, I've got news for you, my girl!'

She gave Jan a vicious shove.

'I can do without the likes of you around here, cosying up to the boss when I've other plans for him. Get out of my sight!'

Rudely she slammed the door.

6

Shocked and upset, Jan ran along the corridor to her bedroom. The woman was insane! Her malevolent attitude gave a whole new meaning to the phrase, bitter and twisted. It made the hair stand up on the back of her neck, but at least she now knew who her enemy was!

Determined to calm herself before going down to have dinner with Raoul, she sat on her bed and took a few deep breaths. Things should have been clearer now that Marta Blignaut had confessed to lying about her father, but they weren't. Thankfully he had been proven innocent of any crime against the Jourdans, so she could relax on that score. Yet she distinctly remembered the tears in his eyes when they'd driven home that day, and men like her father didn't cry easily.

A few days later he had sent her to stay with her grandmother, and then just before her birthday, they'd received the devastating news of his death. It just did not make sense, and until she knew the reason for it she would know no real peace.

She changed her blouse, renewed her make-up and brushed her long blonde hair into a shiny swathe about her shoulders since there wasn't time to pin it up. She sprayed herself with perfume, locked her door and went downstairs to dinner having pinned a convincing smile on her face. Whatever her private worries, she was professional enough to hide them. She was, after all, here to do a job.

Raoul surveyed her for a moment in silence, his calm features hiding the fact that his mouth was dry and his pulse was playing leapfrog. He liked having a woman in the house. He liked the way she looked and the way she moved and the way she spoke, and he wondered what she would look like with that blonde hair fanned out over his pillow.

He was a man who knew what he wanted, and he wanted Jan Harding for his wife. From the moment he'd seen her amongst the daisies he'd been lost. He wondered if she had any idea how much she meant to him. He cleared his throat.

'You look very lovely tonight.'

Jan looked up in surprise.

'Do I? Thank you,' she said, then added a little shyly, 'You don't look too bad yourself, you know.'

It was true. The black roll-neck sweater and dark trousers emphasised his good looks, and something wholly male in the silver eyes disarranged her composure completely.

Raoul seated her next to him before taking his own place at the head of the vast dining-table. He looked every inch the lord of the manor, which made Jan feel even more unsettled. They belonged in different worlds. He needed some debutante from an aristocratic family who could run his ancestral home and fit into his moneyed lifestyle. Yet she couldn't deny she was strongly attracted to the man, which was a ridiculous state of affairs! She was here to do a job, and the sooner she finished it, the sooner she could put space between them and become her own sensible self again.

Sensing her inner turmoil, Raoul set about putting her at ease. They discussed art and music and the latest films as they dined, rising afterwards to take their coffee as usual in one of the sitting-rooms. The French doors were open to reveal a gloriously-warm evening, with dusk settling over the vineyards. Raoul drew Jan to her feet, replaced her empty cup on the tray and suggested that they take a short walk.

He whistled to the dogs who came bounding up. Jan strolled beside him through the garden and out along the road which wound between the vines. She gazed at the mountains, deeply shadowed in the failing light, and gave a sigh of pure pleasure. Hearing it, Raoul draped an arm about her shoulders.

'What are you thinking?'

'Oh, just how marvellous it must be to live here.'

'It is. I am extremely fortunate to have inherited the estate. But there is a lot of responsibility entailed, too, which is why I employ both a farm manager and a cellar master. They ease my work load considerably.'

'Who is the farm manager?'

'Jacques du Toit. He supervises all the maintenance staff.'

At her look of bafflement he explained.

'These are the men who prune, irrigate and spray the vines, not to mention harvesting the grapes at the beginning of each year. You'll meet Jacques. He's a good man.'

'I hardly think so. I'm leaving tomorrow,' Jan reminded him.

'Oh, there'll be other times,' he said casually.

'I doubt it.'

Sans Souci was a beautiful place but

it was not likely to become her stamping ground. In fact, the longer she stayed, the more unsettled she became. Raoul Jourdan, wealthy, sophisticated and doubtless a complete playboy, was in a completely different league.

Overcome with a sudden desire to return to her little cottage and the uncomplicated life she knew, Jan determined to finish her work in record time. She had discovered what she'd come to find, and now that she knew her father had been innocent, she had no further business at Sans Souci. She assumed an interested expression as Raoul obligingly rambled on about how the grapes were harvested at four o'clock in the morning before the warmth of the sun could spoil them.

'We take them by tractor and trailer to the winery where they are loaded into the crusher,' he explained. 'Once the juice is transferred to the sterile, steel tanks, our cellar master then chooses the most suitable yeast for that particular crop. It's a skilful business.

After maturation we bottle the wine ourselves, on the estate.'

They returned to the house where Raoul excused himself, explaining that he had work to do in the study. That suited Jan just fine. At least she'd be away from his disturbing presence.

She worked hard all Friday morning, determined to complete her task by lunchtime so that she could leave immediately afterwards. Fearing a repeat performance of her first evening at Sans Souci, she took the trouble to double check that all her arrangements were perfect before tackling the last one, a particularly pleasing work involving a few artfully-twisted twigs and three silk lilies. Carefully she carried it to the room it was intended for and placed it on the mantelpiece, stepping back to admire its effect. Stunning!

She surveyed the rest of the room with interest. It was one of her favourites, elegant yet cosy, with burgundy and cream striped wallpaper and a collection of comfortable armchairs with plump cushions. The floor was polished and spread with thick, oriental rugs, and there were one or two delicate rosewood cabinets and small lamp tables all holding a variety of porcelain ornaments and silverware. In Jan's book, it was quite perfect!

As she turned to go, a particularly attractive piece of Meissen porcelain caught her eye. It stood on one of the cabinets, a beautiful blue and gold urn, obviously old and valuable. Gently Jan reached out and stroked its smooth surface, longing to pick it up and examine it more closely but not quite daring to do so. When she heard a rustle of cloth behind her, she spun around with a startled gasp. Mrs Blignaut stood a few feet away, staring past her at the vase. There was a fanatical gleam in her black eyes.

'Late nineteenth century,' she murmured, 'a Helena Wolfsohn design, of course. It happens to be one of Mister Raoul's favourite pieces.'

'It's very beautiful,' Jan agreed,

feeling as though she'd been caught with her hand in the cookie jar.

The woman not only irritated her, she positively gave her the creeps. Mrs Blignaut had snapped out of her preoccupied stare and focused her glare upon Jan. There was a positively malevolent gleam in the dark eyes.

'My niece would not wish you to finger the ornaments in this fashion, Miss Harding. Kindly leave this room immediately.'

'Your niece?'

'My late husband's relative, Lisette Blignaut. She arrives next week.'

As though that explained anything, Jan thought, and despite herself she gave in to her curiosity.

'What has your niece to do with Sans Souci?'

The housekeeper sneered triumphantly.

'She will marry Raoul, become mistress here. It is only a matter of time.'

'I didn't know.'

'She is a beautiful girl, extremely clever, and she visits me frequently, so that Raoul has had ample opportunity to fall in love with her. They will marry and have children, and I shall retire. Lisette is a biddable girl. I will direct matters behind the scenes.'

She indicated the door.

'You will remove yourself now, Miss Harding.'

With dignity, Jan took herself to the door. She was just going anyway, couldn't get away fast enough, in fact. Thank goodness she would never have to speak to the awful woman again.

It was only as she stood beside her van that afternoon that Jan realised the true source of her turmoil, jealousy! She was jealous of the unknown Lisette Blignaut, and the reason was clear. Against her better judgment, she had fallen deeply in love with the unattainable Raoul Jourdan, and why she should discover that love at this moment was beyond her!

Raoul stood beside the van, having

obligingly deposited her suitcase and other equipment on the back seat, together with a cardboard wine carrier. Jan thanked him in a polite voice and put out her hand.

'Goodbye, Raoul. I shall send you my bill in due course.'

'No problem.'

He opened her door.

'There's some wine in there for your grandmother, two bottles of Chardonnay and some Pinotage. Please give her my regards.'

'I will. Thank you for your kindness.'

Raoul smiled and bent to kiss her, a casual salute on the cheek which, instead of quickening her heartbeat, left her feeling unaccountably annoyed.

'Goodbye, butterfly lady. It remains for me to thank you for making my home even more beautiful than it already is.'

It really was goodbye, Jan thought sadly as she drove away. Now that she had discovered her love for him, she trembled with that discovery. She had just said goodbye to the only man she wanted, and would most likely never see again. The thought left her even more shaken and unhappy, and all the lovely satisfaction she'd gained from a job well done was swept away.

'Little fool,' Jan reprimanded herself briskly.

The sooner she forgot about him, the happier she'd be. Life must go on, and it would!

Mrs Burney took one look at her granddaughter when she arrived home and noted the strain behind her eyes, but wisely said nothing. The dear child had obviously been working too hard.

'A nice plate of Irish stew and an hour or two in front of the television and you'll soon unwind, Janetta,' she said with brisk commonsense. 'Tomorrow afternoon, once you've shut up shop, we'll take another drive somewhere, shall we?'

Jan kissed her grandmother's cheek and summoned a brief smile.

'Whatever you say, Grandmother.'

The sooner she got on with her life, the better, but it would be easier said than done. She took her suitcase into the bedroom, sat down on the bed and immediately fell to wondering what Raoul was doing.

In fact, Raoul was at that moment enjoying a quiet drink on the terrace before going in to dinner. His expression was grim. His housekeeper had just informed him that a valuable piece of porcelain was missing from the house. He'd followed her to the cosy sitting-room which Jan had liked so much, the room he used to entertain friends after dinner on occasion, and stared in perplexity at the empty space on the rosewood cabinet.

'It was here this morning,' Mrs Blignaut assured him. 'I saw it myself. In fact, I found Miss Harding admiring it. We had a nice chat about it.'

'I see. Are you sure one of the maids hasn't moved it?'

'I've searched the house, sir, and questioned everyone. I'm particularly upset about it because I'm expecting a visit from my niece, Lisette, on Monday, and she's very interested in Meissen pieces. Lisette is very knowledgeable about porcelain, you know, and she has a great love for the contents of Sans Souci. I was hoping to show it to her.'

She allowed the words to hang.

'Perhaps the police should be informed. Do you think Miss Harding . . . '

Raoul's jaw hardened.

'Leave the matter with me, Mrs Blignaut,' he clipped. 'Thank you for reporting it. There is no need to concern yourself any further.'

He finished his drink and took himself into the dining-room where he ate his way through his meal without tasting any of it. It was inconceivable that Jan Harding would stoop to a theft of this nature, but all the evidence pointed in her direction. He had no intention of summoning the police until he had had the opportunity of speaking to her himself, but unfortunately he was giving a talk at a meeting of the Winemakers' Guild in the morning. After that he had promised to spend the rest of the weekend with Antoinette and Paul at Citrusdale. The matter would have to wait until Monday.

With a heavy heart, he took his coffee out on to the terrace and stood drinking it, his eyes fastened on the rows of vines which crept up the slopes of the mountain. Sans Souci meant absolutely nothing to him without the woman he loved, the woman he intended to make his wife.

But what if she turned out to be a thief?

7

Clare Tatham studied Jan, her boss, as she added a foliage filler to the bouquet of summer flowers she was arranging for one of the hospitals in the town. Jan hadn't been herself ever since she'd returned from that assignment at Sans Souci and it was obvious something had upset her, either that or she was in love — with the handsome owner of Sans Souci!

'I hear Mister Jourdan is fabulously wealthy,' she said casually. 'Old money, you know. Did you like his home?'

Jan frowned as she threw a bunch of unusable roses into the bin. She had no wish to be reminded of something she would far rather put behind her, a hopeless endeavour, it seemed, for Raoul's dark, disturbing good looks had continued to haunt her dreams by night and her thoughts by day. Drat the man!

'Well?' Clare prompted.

'No-one can deny that Raoul Jourdan is loaded, Clare. His home is fabulous. He is also charming, good-looking and a very exciting man. There is only one problem.'

'What's that?'

'He's engaged. He's going to marry the niece of that awful housekeeper of his. Apparently she is beautiful and extremely clever.'

'Who told you that?'

'The housekeeper. Look, do we have to talk about this?'

'Of course not,' Clare agreed sympathetically.

She'd been right. Jan was in love with Raoul. What a pity the man was already hooked! Jan was a lovely person and she deserved to have someone special who would make her happy.

The day dragged to a close. Clare departed at two-thirty to collect her daughter and Jan pottered about the shop, smiling determinedly whenever she had cause to approach a customer who needed attention. Life was definitely going to continue and she would forget about Raoul if it killed her, which it probably would! Already a small part of her felt as though it had died. Her thoughts turned at that point to her father. If only she knew why he'd died!

Jan locked the front door of the shop on the dot of five-thirty, relieved to have weathered the day. With any luck and a determined effort on her part, things would get easier as time went by. She let herself out of the back door of the building and walked quickly to her car.

She almost fainted when she saw Raoul. He was leaning against her car with his arms folded across his chest, his face expressionless.

'What are you doing here?' Jan managed to say.

'I thought we'd have a meal somewhere, nothing elaborate.'

'Why?' Jan challenged.

Couldn't the man simply exit her life so that she could get on with it?

'I wish to talk to you.'

Jan threw him an irritated glance.

'Why? I would rather you said whatever you need to say here and now.'

At her tone, Raoul's eyebrows lifted. She was unusually tense, a sign of her guilt, perhaps? He took her arm.

'And I would far rather we took our time over the conversation. Besides, I'm hungry.'

Jan tried again.

'I can't just come out with you at the drop of a hat, Raoul. I have my grandmother to consider. She will already have prepared our evening meal.'

Raoul reached into a pocket for his mobile telephone and thrust it into her hands.

'Phone her.'

With a resigned sigh, Jan did as she was told. The man was determined but she might as well listen to what he had to say because something in his demeanour told her it was important.

And as for his so-called fiancée, if she allowed Raoul to date other women whenever he pleased, then be the results on her own head!

'Grandmother?' she asked, when she made the call.

'Yes, dear.'

'Mister Jourdan has arrived to take me out for a meal tonight. Have you already made the dinner?'

'No, dear,' the old lady lied convincingly. 'You go out and enjoy yourself, Janetta. It's about time you had some fun.'

Jan handed the telephone back, holding her temper in check. This was no date, but she hadn't had the heart to shatter the old lady's illusions.

'Let's go,' she told Raoul. 'I'll go in my own car, if you don't mind.'

Whatever he had to say could surely be said while they had a pre-dinner drink, and then she would leave. She had to confess to a feeling of curiosity about why he was going to all this trouble to speak to her, not to mention the traitorous little desire for an hour of his company.

'As you like.'

Jan did not ask where they were going, and was surprised when he left Stellenbosch behind and drove west, turning off the highway on to an unfamiliar country road which wound between vineyards and strawberry farms. She followed him into the carpark of a small inn which was set well back from the road.

'We'll get a reasonable meal here and the dress is informal,' he explained as he assisted her from her car.

If she were relaxed, she would surely open her heart to him. He badly needed to understand her, to know why she'd so blatantly stolen his property, if that was the case.

Raoul had spent the entire weekend searching his soul, so much so that even his sister, Antoinette, had implored him to pull himself together.

'I don't know what's bugging you, Raoul, but you're walking around like an animal which has lost its mate.'

Which is precisely how he did feel!

He escorted Jan into the cosy lounge of the inn and seated her in a corner where they would have some privacy.

'What will you drink, Jan?'

'Oh, a glass of tonic water with lemon, please.'

She needed to preserve a clear head for whatever it was Raoul was about to say to her. From the grim look in his eyes it was bound to be something unpleasant. She cast back in her mind to try to remember whether she'd neglected any of her duties at Sans Souci. Had she forgotten an arrangement for one of the rooms, perhaps, or made off with the family silver? The outrageous thought brought a reluctant smile to her lips.

Raoul seemed unwilling to broach the subject of whatever was bothering him. He chatted casually about a movie he'd watched on video over the weekend, the state of the economy and the rewards and difficulties of running a large wine estate like Sans Souci.

'We had a veld fire on the mountain above the vineyards one year,' he told her, 'and lost five hectares of Chardonnay grapes.'

Jan assumed polite interest, wishing he'd get to the point of the evening.

'The heat from the hills came down and ripened the grapes more quickly on the outside, leaving the insides green. We salvaged what we could, but it made for a bitter wine.'

He led her into the dining-room, ordered their meal and returned to the subject nearest his heart.

'What did you think of my home?'

Jan tasted her tomato soup before replying in a cautious manner. No need to gush over something you had no wish to see again!

'I liked it very much.'

'Did you have an opportunity to examine the rooms at some length?'

'Oh, yes. I studied each room thoroughly before I decided on the arrangement which would suit it best.'

'Yes, of course.'

Raoul waited until the waitress had taken away the empty bowls before continuing.

'Mrs Blignaut tells me that you and she had a little chat about one of the Meissen pieces you were examining in the small sitting-room.'

Jan went as rosy as the soup she'd just eaten.

'Yes.'

She remembered the way Mrs Blignaut had caught her stroking that vase, and how unnecessarily guilty she'd been made to feel. The memory of it still caused her embarrassment, as though she'd had designs on the thing! Raoul was watching her intently. The various expressions which flitted across her face only served to confirm his worst fears. She'd definitely stolen the vase. He sighed heavily.

'Why did you do it, Jan?'

Why had she examined the vase? What an odd question!

'Well, I liked it,' she explained

133

reasonably. 'It's a very attractive piece, isn't it? It must be extremely valuable.'

'Extremely,' he agreed dryly, adding, 'it should fetch a lot of money at Sotheby's.'

'Is it insured?'

'Naturally.'

'Well, there's no need to worry about it then, is there?'

Raoul stared at her in amazement. She was so blasé about it!

'No,' he agreed bitterly, 'there isn't.'

He had already decided that should he discover her to be guilty he would not go to the police. He would not claim from the insurance company, either. He would write off the loss just as he would write off Jan Harding. He'd delete the whole episode from his mind. He smiled grimly. Unfortunately, he was one of those individuals who loved with an all-forgiving kind of love. He would write the whole episode off to bitter experience and he would never, ever allow himself to be caught in this manner again. He would get on with his life and consign Jan Harding to the daisies if he could.

'Why is it so important to you that I liked your vase so much?' Jan asked curiously as she tackled her steak pie.

Raoul could not believe his ears.

'Important to me? Good heavens, girl,' he grated, 'who wouldn't be interested to find out why someone you liked and trusted had stolen one of your belongings?'

Jan stared at him in consternation.

'I don't understand. Who stole what?'

'You did,' he snapped. 'You took the Meissen vase from Sans Souci.'

Jan laid down her fork and looked at him incredulously.

'Let's get this straight. You think I stole your crummy ornament?'

'Isn't it the truth?'

'No!'

'Come off it, Jan,' he scoffed. 'You're obviously guilty, and acting as cool as they come about it.'

Jan stood up.

'You are completely mistaken,' she

told him coldly. 'I did not steal your wretched vase and I have no intention of putting up with any more of this unspeakable nonsense. Goodbye, Raoul. Thank you for the dinner, and I hope I never see you again.'

Angrily she snatched up her handbag and marched out of the inn. Raoul sat for a moment, his thoughts bleak. And goodbye to you, too, butterfly lady, he thought sadly.

Jan drove home in record time, at a complete loss to know why Raoul had accused her of theft in such an extraordinary way. Had he been drinking before he'd arrived at the shop? She couldn't believe it. He wasn't that type of man. Anyway, whatever the reason, she wanted nothing further to do with him, ever.

Mrs Burney was watching television in the sitting-room when Jan arrived home.

'Oh, is that you, dear? You're back rather soon. I was expecting . . . '

She took one look at Jan's face and

decided not to pursue the subject.

'Would you like a cup of cocoa, dear?'

'I'll make it,' Jan told her and disappeared into the kitchen.

Mrs Burney sighed. Obviously the outing had not gone well but hopefully it wouldn't be too long before they had another visit from Raoul Jourdan, and then all would be well. A little break from each other would do them good. As the saying went, absence made the heart grow fonder. As long as it wasn't a case of out of sight, out of mind.

But all was not well, she was forced to admit when after two weeks her granddaughter was still walking around with an unhappy air. The girl had lost weight, too. She was in love, anyone could see that, but the object of her affections did not appear to be behaving as he ought. He was neglecting her dear Janetta. Perhaps all he needed was a little encouragement.

She waited until Jan had left for work next morning before hauling out the telephone directory and dialling the estate office at Sans Souci.

'I would like to speak with Mister Raoul Jourdan, please,' she said firmly.

Raoul's secretary asked who was calling.

'Tell him it is Daffodil Burney.'

A moment later Raoul's voice came tersely down the line.

'Daffodil? How may I help you?'

She was taken aback. He sounded so businesslike.

'I hope I haven't called at a busy time. I should like you to come to dinner one evening, Raoul,' she said. 'Will Saturday do?'

There was a moment's silence.

'I'm afraid that would be quite impossible,' he informed her smoothly.

'Oh? Another evening, then?'

'It is extremely kind of you, Mrs Burney, but I will not be available.'

His tone said, now or ever, quite definitely.

Thoughtfully Mrs Burney replaced the receiver. She was nothing but a meddling, old woman who had allowed herself a few foolish fantasies! It was perfectly obvious the man had no interest whatever in her granddaughter or he'd have jumped at the opportunity to see her again. This, then, was the reason for poor Janetta's glum face these days. She would be hard put not to bear a glum face herself, after this disappointment. Funny, she'd been so sure he'd been very taken with Jan.

She went into the kitchen, poked around in the cupboards and decided to make a Pavlova for dessert that evening, with lashings of cream and fresh fruit. Jan had always liked Pavlova. It would cheer them both up.

Back at Sans Souci, Raoul replaced the receiver thoughtfully. He hadn't liked to give the dear old lady the brush-off like that, but he'd made up his mind to cut them out of his life, and that was that. For the remainder of the day he applied himself diligently to estate business and returned to the homestead in time to take a shower before dinner. Lisette Blignaut was dining with him tonight.

A charming girl, he thought as he buttoned himself into a crisp white shirt. Her aunt, Mrs Blignaut, had been hinting for days that Lisette would like to dine with him, but he'd been too busy to comply until this evening. He shrugged into his dinner jacket and took himself downstairs. It was a warm evening and they would take their drinks out on the terrace. From the corner of his eye he noticed that Mrs Blignaut was hovering about the hall, and frowned.

She should have gone off duty. The woman was beginning to bother him profoundly. He couldn't say what it was, exactly, but she seemed to bring an unfortunate atmosphere wherever she went, and there had been one or two complaints from the staff. She was excellent at her job, but perhaps he should begin looking for another housekeeper.

Lisette Blignaut arrived, all smiles, in

a cloud of floral perfume. She was a dark, pretty girl, with melting brown eyes and bewitching dimples in her plump cheeks. He could quite see why Jacques du Toit was so taken with her. He stood up and kissed her lightly on the cheek.

'Hello, Lisette.'

'Raoul, am I glad to be given this opportunity to see you. You're so busy these days. I've been trying to get together with you all week.'

He apologised and offered her a glass of wine.

'Thank you. Do you have a Sauvignon Blanc 1997?'

'Ah, I see my farm manager has been educating you well. That was our best vintage to date,' he observed.

Lisette blushed.

'Oh, yes, Jacques certainly is a good teacher.'

Raoul handed her a crystal wine glass.

'Try that.'

Lisette took a sip.

'Lovely, and to think that so much work has gone into the making of it. I'm told the men work for forty-eight hours on end once the harvesting and crushing begins.'

Raoul put down his own glass and got straight to the point.

'What is it you wanted to see me about, Lisette?'

'Well, I need your advice, as usual. You've always been like a big brother to me, Raoul. With my parents both dead, I have only my aunt to advise me, and she's a little . . . '

She broke off, embarrassed.

'Well, she's not exactly my cup of tea.'

This was news to Raoul.

'You don't get on?'

'Oh, we get on, providing I agree with everything she says. To be honest, I find her a little strange. My father always said she was not to be trusted. He couldn't understand what his brother had seen in her in the first place.'

'How long is it that you've been coming here?'

'Oh, years. I've spent almost every school holiday with my aunt, but usually I couldn't wait to get back to school. I don't know how she can enjoy a job like housekeeping. It would drive me nuts. Not,' she added hurriedly, 'that Sans Souci is an unpleasant place to live, but give me a small cottage any day, and I'll be perfectly happy. A cottage like Jacques', actually.'

'Ah, yes, Jacques. What is the news on that front?'

Lisette's eyes sparkled.

'He has asked me to marry him.'

'Has he, indeed? The man has gained some sense, at last.'

She laughed.

'He did rather take his time about asking me, but I'm worth waiting for.'

Raoul smiled.

'I won't argue with that. What's the problem then?'

Lisette's smile disappeared.

'I'm not sure I'll make him a good

enough wife. I don't think I'm cut out to be a farmer's wife. I've always lived in a city, haven't I? Cape Town's a pretty exciting place. What if I miss it too much?'

'Do you love him, Lisette?'

'Very much.'

'Then your love is surely strong enough to overcome this difficulty. You will both have to make the necessary adjustments. Jacques will have to see to it that he takes you wining and dining occasionally, and you'll have to make sure you have enough to do on the estate to keep you from being bored. Why not take a little job in Franschhoek? You like antiques. You could find something in one of the shops there. If you want something badly enough, you'll find a way.'

'You make it all sound so uncomplicated.'

'It is uncomplicated. The only thing which really matters is your love for each other. Believe me.'

Something in his voice caused her to

look at him curiously.

'You sound as though you're in love yourself, Raoul.'

He finished his drink.

'Do I?'

He set the glass down with elaborate care and said blandly, 'If you're ready, we'll go in to dinner.'

Afterwards they took their after-dinner coffee in the small sitting-room. Eventually Lisette stood up to go.

'Thank you for a lovely evening, Raoul, and for the advice.'

She glanced around the room appreciatively.

'Speaking of antiques, you have some lovely Meissen, and it was very kind of you to give my aunt that blue and gold vase.'

Raoul's head snapped up.

'Vase? Which vase?'

Lisette indicated with one graceful arm.

'You know, the one which used to stand on that cabinet over there.'

'Would you repeat that, Lisette?'

She looked puzzled.

'The vase. My aunt said you gave it to her and it now has pride of place in her sitting-room, but for some reason or other she told me not to tell anybody about it. Said you'd be annoyed if you knew the other staff members knew, something about causing jealousy, and I can quite see that. I haven't breathed a word. Anyway, I just wanted to say that I thought it was very generous of you.'

She reached up and kissed him on the cheek.

'Thanks again for everything. I'm going right now to see Jacques, to put him out of his misery.'

Lisette departed in a happy whirl, flinging excitedly over her shoulder, 'The next time you see me I'll be wearing a great big rock on my finger.'

Raoul went to the cabinet to pour himself a stiff drink, which he took out on to the veranda where he sat, deep in thought. In the morning, he would be forced to pay his housekeeper a little visit . . .

8

Marta Blignaut stared at her niece in angry disbelief when they met next morning, after Lisette's visit to Jacques.

'I'm engaged to be married to Jacques du Toit,' Lisette repeated. 'Will you wish me well?'

'No, I will not! You are a tiresome girl,' her aunt burst out. 'I will do no such thing.'

Lisette's happy smile died.

'Why ever not?'

'Ungrateful wretch!'

'I'm not ungrateful for what you've done, Aunt Marta. I would have thought you'd be happy. I'll be living on the estate and I'll be able to see you more often. I can't understand why you're reacting like this!'

Mrs Blignaut went an unbecoming puce.

'I will not stand by and see you

marry that farm boy! I won't have you spoiling my plans for the future, for our future.'

'Jacques is no boy,' Lisette protested. 'He's a very attractive man and he loves me and I'm going to marry him, whatever you think. Anyway, I don't understand. What plans have I spoiled?'

'I had decided that you will marry Raoul Jourdan.'

Lisette's pretty mouth fell open.

'What did you say?'

'You will marry him and you will make a fine mistress of Sans Souci.'

'What rubbish, Aunt,' Lisette said. 'I have no interest in marrying Raoul Jourdan. He doesn't love me. Besides, he's far too old. I'm only twenty-one! I don't love him, either. I love Jacques. My mind is quite made up, Aunt, so it is no use trying to persuade me otherwise.'

'Love! There is no such thing,' Mrs Blignaut declared, giving her niece a furious glare. 'You will leave this house immediately. I never wish to set eyes on you again. I thought you were a biddable girl. I can see that you are nothing but a headstrong, little fool!'

Lisette viewed her aunt sadly.

'I'm afraid you have been deluding yourself. I shall marry Jacques du Toit and I shall be very happy, and you will be welcome to visit us in our cottage at any time. Goodbye, Aunt Marta.'

When she had gone, Mrs Blignaut looked about her for something to throw. She grabbed Jan's arrangement of flowers from the hall table and hurled it against the wall.

'It's all because of her!' she hissed. 'He has eyes for no-one but the Harding girl.'

She gave vent to a scream of fury. Raoul, on his way to the study, heard the scream. He took the stairs two at a time and flung open the door of his housekeeper's apartment. His voice was like ice.

'Good morning, Mrs Blignaut.'

She glared at him.

'I shall begin my duties in a minute.

What do you want?'

'Oh, I think you know, Mrs Blignaut.'

He strode into her small sitting-room, glanced about him and quickly found what he was looking for.

'You informed me that this vase was missing, Mrs Blignaut, yet you have been hiding it away in your living-room. Why?'

Mrs Blignaut glowered.

'I did it for Lisette,' she told him defiantly.

'I require more of an explanation than that.'

'Lisette was to marry you and become mistress of Sans Souci, instead of that . . . that miss!' she spat out.

'What miss?'

'The Harding girl. She doesn't belong here, she's nothing but . . . ' She sought for the right word. 'Pond scum!'

With a supreme effort, Raoul controlled his feelings.

'Let me get this straight. You deliberately tried to incriminate Miss Harding so that your niece would be in the running as mistress of this house?'

'Lisette would have made a beautiful bride,' she told him wrathfully. 'She'd have run Sans Souci to perfection.'

'With you at her right hand,' Raoul grated, his tones dangerously quiet. 'I shall not call in the police, Mrs Blignaut, for the simple reason it would result in adverse publicity for Sans Souci, with every tabloid in the country baying for a story, and that I will not tolerate. I will, however, suspend you from your duties with immediate effect. You will accept a cheque in lieu of notice and you will leave these premises by midday tomorrow.'

Mrs Blignaut's face crumpled.

'But where shall I go?' she whined.

'That is for you to decide.'

She drew herself up to her full height.

'I shall go to my sister, and I will never forgive your unjust treatment of me, Raoul Jourdan. I have served you faithfully for many years.'

'With the ulterior motive of one day

becoming surrogate mistress of my home,' Raoul said. 'I'm afraid you have made a very grave error of judgement, Mrs Blignaut. I have no sympathy for you.'

'I did it for Lisette,' she retorted.

'No, Mrs Blignaut,' Raoul corrected coldly, 'you did it for yourself.'

He went back to his study and picked up the telephone. He would instruct his secretary to find another housekeeper at the earliest convenience, and in the meantime he was confident that the staff knew their jobs well enough to function without supervision, at least for a few days. He took a deep breath, lifted the receiver once more and dialled the number which had been pencilled on his blotter for weeks.

'Mrs Burney? This is Raoul Jourdan.'

He listened to her gasp of surprise and smiled before continuing.

'I find that I am free this week, after all. May I take you up on your kind invitation to have dinner?'

Daffodil Burney beamed.

'Why, of course, dear boy, it would be a pleasure. Which night would suit you?'

Raoul cleared his throat.

'Would tonight do?'

'Certainly. Seven-thirty sharp.'

She put down the telephone and did a small jig around the hall so that Tiger, busy with his ablutions on the chair next to the telephone, was compelled to pause and stare.

'We shall do our Jan proud, my feline friend,' Mrs Burney assured him firmly. 'Now then. I shall go and see what I can find in the freezer.'

★   ★   ★

Jan, hearing a slight commotion, paused in the middle of arranging a vase of fresh gladioli and went to serve the customer in the red dress. The woman was insisting loudly that the roses she wanted to buy were far too expensive and there was too much greenery in the arrangement. Clare, her face as red as

153

the dress, cast Jan a speaking look and took herself to the back to find something more suitable.

'Is there a problem?' Jan asked pleasantly.

'Are you the owner?'

'Yes, I am. How may I help you?'

'You should know better than to charge such prices,' the woman complained belligerently. 'I need yellow roses for my mother but I'm not paying that much. It's a disgrace!'

Jan hadn't been in this job for two years for nothing. She recognised stress when she saw it.

'Your mother is ill?' she asked gently.

The woman's mouth trembled.

'She's dying. Now tell your assistant to hurry up. I must get to the hospital.'

Clare returned with another arrangement of roses.

'Unfortunately there is nothing smaller, madam. Will this do?' she asked politely.

'How much?'

'There will be no charge,' Jan

intervened firmly.

The woman's mouth dropped open.

'No charge?'

'That's right. Do visit us again, and I hope your mother gets well soon.'

The woman gave her a tremulous smile.

'I certainly will call again, and I'll tell all my friends. Thank you very much.'

'One satisfied customer,' Clare murmured as the woman left the shop.

'Yes, but I didn't do it so that she would tell her friends, you know,' Jan said.

'I know. You're one sweet lady, Jan Harding. It's been a heck of a day, hasn't it?'

Jan sighed.

'Yes. You go off now if you like, Clare. I can manage.'

By five-thirty, Jan felt wrung out. The heat had been unbearable, a sign of things to come as a delightful spring melted into a hot summer. She would have to start storing her flowers in the cool room if this heat persisted.

She locked up, thankful that tomorrow was Saturday. For some reason she'd been feeling a distinct lack of motivation all week, and for the first time ever had thought of selling the shop. But what would she do with herself? The answer came immediately. She would give herself to her painting, even exhibit her work in galleries, but she needed to support her grandmother, and they couldn't exist on the income from her painting alone.

She sighed as she inserted the key into the ignition. If she kept on going through the motions, life would continue as it had been before she'd met Raoul, minus the joy, but that would surely return in time. The trouble was, she knew she could never be truly happy without him.

Jan turned into her driveway and cast an idle glance across the street at the vehicle parked there. The Potters must be having visitors, she thought. For a moment she'd imagined it to be Raoul's car. It was the same make.

'Do pull yourself together,' she ordered sternly.

It was no good wishing for the moon, so the quicker she got said moon out of her mind, the better. The kitchen smelled heavenly as she entered.

'Hello, Gran, I'm home. What's for dinner?'

'Roast beef and yorkshire pudding, with roast potatoes, sprouts and glazed carrots from the garden. Would you make one of your hazelnut Heavens for afters, love? I can't think of anything I'd like better.'

Jan would have dearly loved to refuse, put her feet up and drink copious cups of tea, but how could she refuse to shoulder her share when her grandmother had been slaving over the main course all afternoon?

'Sure. Just give me five minutes to have a shower.'

She put on the coolest thing she could find in her wardrobe, a sleeveless, deceptively simple designer dress in ocean colours. On impulse she fastened on silver hoop earrings, twisted her hair into an artfully casual knot and thrust he feet into matching low-heeled sandals.

In the kitchen, she found her recipe book, grated the hazelnuts for the mousse and spent the next half hour happily engrossed in her other creative interest — cooking. She peeped into the dining-room on her way to the sitting-room for a cup of tea, and stopped dead in her tracks. There were three place settings, with a fancy seafood starter at each place! Grand-mother had said nothing about them having a guest for dinner. It must be someone special, too, for her to have gone to so much trouble.

'Who is our guest?' she asked as she handed her grandmother a cup of her favourite redbush tea.

'Oh, that nice man, Raoul Jourdan,' Mrs Burney said casually.

Jan choked. She coughed and coughed, and was forced to wait until her breath returned before demanding hotly, 'What on earth possessed you to ask him?'

'I didn't, dear, he asked himself,' her grandmother explained placidly.

Jan gasped.

'Good grief. When was this?'

'He telephoned this morning. I could hardly say no, could I?'

Jan's heartbeat became completely disorganised.

'The man has a nerve!' she muttered fiercely.

'Not at all, dear. We owe him something after that fine afternoon he gave us at Sans Souci.'

'Grandmother, we owe him nothing!' Jan retorted.

She reflected bitterly that if Raoul had invited himself to dinner, it must be for a very good reason. He would probably tell her that he wanted to press charges against her for stealing his vase. It was outrageous! At the very thought her cheeks bloomed indignantly. She had a good mind to excuse herself and drive off to a café for her meal, only she was not a girl to back down from a challenge. If Raoul Jourdan wished to make unsubstantiated allegations he must prove them. And if he wanted a fight, he'd get it!

'That's a very becoming outfit,' her grandmother remarked.

And I hope it knocks Raoul dead, Jan thought. Let him drool! After this evening he could go back to his fiancée and she would never see him again, but at least she would have given the man something to remember her by.

Mrs Burney sipped her tea and allowed herself a small, satisfied smile.

'Open the red wine, will you, dear, so that it can breathe?' she asked.

'I've already done so, Grandmother. At least we'll be able to offer our guest the very best.'

'Yes. There's nothing quite like Sans Souci wines. Ah, there's the doorbell now. Would you let him in, please, Jan?'

Jan nodded. She went into the hall,

conscious of the pot pourri of emotions fluttering within her, excitement, bewilderment, anger. She flung open the door with a cool smile.

'Hello, Raoul.'

At the sight of her, Raoul's breath caught. He greeted her blandly.

'Janetta.'

'Please, come in. Grandmother has been looking forward to seeing you again.'

Not we have been looking forward to seeing you, he thought ruefully. He could hardly blame her. He'd made a fool of himself at their last meeting and it behoved him to put the record straight as soon as possible, if she would give him that opportunity, that is. Judging by the look in her eyes, she would prefer him to drop dead.

Raoul greeted Mrs Burney with friendly warmth, thanked her for allowing him to come to dinner and engaged her in placid conversation. Jan, watching him, gave an unconscious sigh. It was a great pity he was engaged to that Blignaut woman's niece. She would lead him a dance, and between the two obnoxious women they would make his life a misery. For a moment her kind heart contracted at the thought.

They had just embarked on the dessert when Mrs Burney asked innocently if he found the mousse to his liking.

'It's wonderful,' Raoul told her appreciatively and added, much to the old lady's delight, 'Would you be so kind as to let me have the recipe for my cook?'

Mrs Burney beamed.

'You shall have it, dear, but you must ask Janetta. She made it. She's a very good cook, you know.'

Raoul turned to stare at Jan.

'No, I didn't know. But then, we don't know much about one another, do we, Jan?'

'And that's the way it is likely to stay,' Jan told him sweetly.

'I shall make the coffee. You two go

into the sitting-room,' Mrs Burney urged.

Jan would have liked to have refused. This was just what she'd hoped to avoid because, apart from the vase episode, she and Raoul Jourdan had nothing to say to each other.

'Jan,' he began at once, when they were alone.

Jan's eyes were cold.

'Yes, Raoul?' she said in tones as cold as ice.

'I owe you an enormous apology. I was completely wrong in my allegations about you concerning that vase which disappeared. It has been found and safely returned.'

This was definitely not what she'd been expecting.

'I'm very pleased to hear it. It is a beautiful vase, and much too valuable to lose.'

'Am I forgiven?'

She glared at him.

'I will forget the episode, yes,' she said, thinking, in the same way she

163

would forget him.

Raoul gave a rueful smile.

'Thank you. I should very much like to continue where we left off. Will you allow me to take you out to dinner tomorrow evening?'

'No,' Jan told him baldly. 'I'm afraid that would be impossible.'

If the man thought he could accuse her of theft and then expect everything to be all right, he was mistaken. Anyway, he was engaged to be married. She might have many faults, but stealing another woman's man was not one of them.

Raoul studied her stony face with narrowed eyes.

'May I ask why?'

'I do not have to give reasons, but just so there can be no confusion, let me say one thing. I'm not interested in you or your wine estate. After this evening is over I would ask you not to contact us again, ever.'

9

Mrs Blignaut departed from Sans Souci the following morning amidst much bluster and many dark mutterings about taking legal advice. Raoul's head gardener helped her carry her belongings to the hired van and saw her off the property before going to the staff dining-room for his morning tea. He was greeted by a number of happy faces.

'She's gone? Good riddance,' Susanne said boldly.

'Let's hope we get someone reasonable in her place,' Magda remarked. 'Mister Raoul doesn't need any domestic hassles. He has enough on his hands as it is.'

'What he needs is a wife. Someone like that nice young lady who arranged the flowers.'

'Yes, but she's not likely to come here

again. She couldn't wait to get away fast enough, what with Mrs Blignaut always breathing down her neck, and the way someone deliberately messed with that flower arrangement. I'll bet it was that woman.'

'Well,' Susanne opined, 'I just hope Mister Raoul finds somebody nice to cheer him up. The man has a face like a thundercloud this morning.'

Raoul, sitting at his desk, swallowed his coffee, picked up a file and informed his secretary as he strode through the foyer that he was going to see Jacques du Toit about the new irrigation system. He found Jacques instructing the labourers at one end of the vineyard and spent the next ten minutes discussing work. As he turned to go he thrust out his hand.

'I believe congratulations are in order, Jacques. I had dinner with Lisette the other night and she told me you two are to be married.'

His farm manager gave a happy grin. 'That's right, Raoul. I must thank you for putting in a good word at the right time. Lisette has now gone back to Cape Town to prepare for our wedding. I'm sorry about her aunt, and that unpleasant business about the vase. I can't say I'm sorry to see the back of the woman. She'd been a constant thorn in our sides. Funny how some people cause unhappiness wherever they go! Have you had any luck with a new housekeeper?'

Raoul shrugged.

'My secretary says she has a couple of applicants lined up for interviews next week. I daresay we'll find a suitable replacement.'

He took himself back to the office where he sat for a moment in thought. Despite her obvious hostility towards him he was convinced Jan was not as immune to him as she would have him believe. He was determined to pursue his butterfly lady and make her his own, and nothing in all the world would deflect him from his purpose. All it needed was some careful thought and planning, but for the life of him he could think of nothing at this precise moment. He would give her some space for a week or two, and then decide how to conduct his campaign of action.

★ ★ ★

Jan sat on the patio sipping a tall glass of orange juice while her grandmother poured herself another cup of tea.

'It's been a lovely day, hasn't it?' the old lady commented. 'I enjoyed the church service this morning.'

'Yes. Grandmother,' Jan said slowly, 'may I ask you something?'

'Of course, dear.'

'It's something which has worried me for a long time now. I've never spoken about it because I didn't want to reopen any old wounds for you, but there is something I simply must know.'

'Yes, dear, what is it?' her grand-mother asked kindly.

'Why did my father take his life?'

Mrs Burney put down her cup and stared.

'But, Janetta, I thought you knew!'

'Knew what?'

'Your father had been diagnosed with an incurable illness and had only weeks to live, if even that. He left a note begging us to forgive him, but he felt it was something he had to do in order to spare us the pain of watching him deteriorate. He knew what we'd suffered seeing your mother die, you see, and he didn't want us to go through it all a second time.'

Jan felt her eyes become moist.

'Poor Daddy. No-one ever explained it to me.'

'In a way it was a brave thing to do, although I can never condone suicide. It is not for us to take our own or another person's life.'

Jan gave a great sigh of relief.

'Thank you for telling me, Grandmother. I hope I haven't upset you.'

'No, my dear. I'm sorry you have had to wonder all these years. I'd have told you if I'd known.'

Jan stood up to make more tea. She felt as though the burden she'd carried for so long had been lifted, and the world was a kinder place because of it. Despite his actions, she would always remember her father as the fine, honourable man he was.

'It's all right, Grandmother, truly it is,' she said.

Jan was alone in the shop the following Saturday, having allowed Clare to depart half an hour early in order to collect her daughter from a friend's house. She looked up as the bell pinged and an attractive, dark-haired young woman entered the shop. She approached the counter with an enthusiastic smile.

'Good morning. I'm told you are an expert at wedding flowers. May I see your brochure, please?'

'Certainly. Take a seat over there while you look it over. Would you like a cup of coffee?' Jan offered.

'Oh, yes, please.'

She left the posy she was finishing off and went to switch on the kettle. She had a number of weddings lined up and would be very busy during the summer months, but the busier she was, the more she liked it. It kept her from dreaming hopeless dreams about a certain man she'd met not so long ago in a field of daisies.

'When is the wedding to be?' she enquired as she placed a tray on the small table between two chairs in a corner of the shop.

The girl grinned.

'I'm afraid we are in rather a hurry. Neither of us can wait. We've wasted so much time already. We plan to marry in two weeks' time, that is why I'm rushing about trying to organise everything. But it's fun, isn't it?'

She glanced through the brochure.

'I like this bouquet, here. Just the one bouquet, no bridesmaids, and of course a buttonhole for my groom, and the flowers in the reception room at the hotel, and one large arrangement in the church. It is to be a very small wedding, so we shan't need much. Do say you will help me. I've heard such good reports of you.'

Jan warmed to the girl.

'Two weeks?'

She consulted the large diary on the counter.

'Yes, I can help you. Now as to cost.'

She discussed the fee and asked where the bridal bouquet was to be delivered to.

'Oh, don't bother, we can fetch it, just let me know when. I'll be staying in the main house at Sans Souci, a wine estate near Franschhoek. You may have heard of it. My fiancé lives there.'

Jan went white.

'I see. And your name is?'

She knew it without being told.

'Lisette Blignaut.'

Raoul Jourdan's fiancée! Of all the awful luck, that she should be asked to do the flowers for his wedding. She could always refuse and make some excuse, of course, but she would not turn tail and run. Besides, she had just given her word. And strangely enough, she rather liked this Lisette Blignaut.

'You're looking rather pale,' Lisette observed in a concerned voice. 'It's this frightful heat, I daresay.'

Quickly Jan pulled herself together. She had a commission to fulfil and she would be as professional about it as always.

'Oh, I'm fine. It is hot today, isn't it?' She added casually, 'Blignaut. I know the name. My parents used to live on the Sans Souci estate, and I once met a Marta Blignaut.'

Lisette looked astounded.

'Did you? My goodness, it's a small world, isn't it? She's my aunt. She used to be the housekeeper there.'

'Used to be?' Jan asked sharply.

Lisette shrugged.

'There was some unpleasantness, and she was asked to leave recently. She was rather a strange person, my aunt.'

I'll say, Jan thought. She plunged

hastily into the merits of lily-of-the-valley versus orange blossom, a subject which occupied them for the next few minutes while Jan decided that the more she saw of Lisette Blignaut, the more she liked her. The two of them could have become friends under different circumstances, but a friendship between them now was completely untenable because they both loved the same man.

The day of Lisette's wedding dawned clear and bright, with a hot sun climbing in the sky. By nine o'clock, Jan was longing for a long, cool drink. She had been up since five o'clock that morning, working very hard, and she had begun to feel the heat. Fortunately, she'd driven to Franschhoek to arrange the church flowers the previous afternoon, and had sprayed them with a fine mist of water before she left so that they would last.

The bridal bouquet had been collected from the shop by one of the estate workers only that morning. He handed Jan an envelope and hurried off before she could furnish him with a reply. It contained a scrawled note from Lisette.

Dear Jan, I would love you to share in my happiness, so please feel free to stay for the reception if you can. It's all rather informal and it would be lovely to see you.

No way, Jan thought. She could never sit through an occasion where the man she loved had just promised to love and cherish someone else. However, she had reckoned without a flat tyre on the way to Franschhoek so that, hot and bothered, she arrived at the hotel with only half an hour to spare.

Feverishly, she worked to set the large arrangement in place. Fortunately she had already made up the centre-piece for the bridal table, and lifted it carefully from its box. She placed it in position and stepped back to admire her handiwork. It had been a close thing, but she had managed!

She gathered up her equipment and

went to find a brush and pan to sweep up the odd piece of foliage on the floor, and then hurried to dispose of the waste. On the way back, she slipped into the powder room to tidy herself just as the first guests appeared in the foyer.

With any luck she could leave the hotel before Raoul and his bride arrived. She had no doubt Lisette would be radiant, because any woman fortunate enough to marry a man like that would be glowing with happiness, but she had no wish to witness it.

Jan paused in the doorway of the reception room, standing politely to one side in order to allow the guests through. When a large hand tightened on her arm, she turned around in irritation. It was hot enough as it was, without being mauled by some over-enthusiastic guest!

'Hello, butterfly lady,' Raoul said quietly.

Jan could only stare, because her heart had lodged itself awkwardly in her throat and normal speech was quite impossible.

Raoul took his time surveying her beautiful face. He gave a slow smile.

'This must be my lucky day,' he said, his voice roughening.

She was even more lovely than ever.

Jan found her tongue at last, and eyed him in disgust.

'You're despicable!'

The man was a compulsive flirt! He ought to have eyes for his bride only. It was his wedding day, for goodness' sake!

Raoul's eyes narrowed.

'Isn't it time we dispensed with hostilities, Jan? I have apologised for my error of judgment over the vase. May we start over again?'

Jan was almost speechless.

'Start again?' she spat out. 'You should be ashamed of yourself. You've only just got yourself married and already you're chatting up another female! I'm getting out of here.'

Uncaring, she pushed past a large

woman in the doorway and ran through the foyer to the hotel entrance, just in time to see Lisette walking up the steps on the arm of her smiling groom, Jacques du Toit! Jan stopped dead, her eyes widening in disbelief. Lisette and Raoul's farm manager? It couldn't be!

She turned around in consternation, only to cannon straight into Raoul. His arms closed about her so that escape was impossible. His gaze, as it took in her flushed, bewildered face, was inscrutable.

'What was all that about my chatting up another female?' he demanded. 'There's only one female I want, Janetta, and it's you. I love only you. Haven't you realised that yet?'

Jan's mouth dropped open.

'But . . . I thought you were marrying Lisette today.'

'Now where did you get that idiotic idea?'

'Mrs Blignaut.'

'Ah. That explains a lot. I knew there had to be a reason for all that verbal abuse. But let's forget the unspeakable woman and move out of the way so that our happy friends can make their way to their wedding reception.'

He marched her down the path to the shrubbery alongside the building, unconcerned about the amused, knowing glances cast their way by Lisette and Jacques as they went inside.

'Where are you taking me?' Jan demanded.

'To a place where I can be assured of a little privacy while I kiss you,' Raoul said with a grin.

He proceeded to carry out his intention with great thoroughness.

'Let us dispense with dithering,' he said at length. 'I'm a man who knows exactly what he wants. Will you make me the happiest wine farmer in South Africa and do me the honour of becoming the mistress of Sans Souci, the mother of my children and the queen of my heart?' he asked.

'Typical Frenchman,' Jan mocked. 'There's no need to be flowery. That's my prerogative.'

'All right, then,' he amended with a twinkle. 'Will you marry me, butterfly lady?'

Jan heaved a great sigh. Suddenly her world had righted itself.

'If it pleases you, kind sir,' she told him, and just in case he hadn't understood, she decided to make it perfectly clear. 'Yes, grasshopper man, I'll marry you.'

Raoul kissed her.

'I have no objection to your continuing to run a business,' he assured her. 'I will even buy you a shop in Franschhoek if you would prefer not to commute to Stellenbosch each day. It's up to you.'

'Well, now that you mention it, I've been thinking. I shall sell Jan's Blooms and spend my days painting flowers.'

'Whatever makes you happy,' Raoul murmured. 'We'll set up a studio for you.'

'There's just one more thing,' Jan told him firmly when she had her breath back. 'Marry me, marry my grandmother.'

'Naturally. Sans Souci is large enough to accommodate ten grandmothers. We'll install Daffodil in a fine apartment at Sans Souci where she can be on hand to keep us all in line, or if she'd prefer it, I can make available a cottage on the estate. No doubt she'll enjoy recommending our fine wines to all the customers, not to mention undertaking the odd bit of babysitting from time to time when I wish to take my wife on a romantic weekend.'

Jan wasn't listening. A faraway look had entered her beautiful eyes.

'I wonder what blooms I should have in my bridal bouquet?' she mused. 'Small, creamy arums, and tiny rosebuds, and lily-of-the-valley, and . . . '

Raoul cut off her musings with a quick kiss.

'And daisies,' he finished with a grin.

We do hope that you have enjoyed reading this large print book.

Did you know that all of our titles are available for purchase?

We publish a wide range of high quality large print books including:
Romances, Mysteries, Classics
General Fiction
Non Fiction and Westerns

Special interest titles available in large print are:
The Little Oxford Dictionary
Music Book, Song Book
Hymn Book, Service Book

Also available from us courtesy of Oxford University Press:
Young Readers' Dictionary
(large print edition)
Young Readers' Thesaurus
(large print edition)

For further information or a free brochure, please contact us at:
Ulverscroft Large Print Books Ltd.,
The Green, Bradgate Road, Anstey,
Leicester, LE7 7FU, England.
Tel: (00 44) **0116 236 4325**
Fax: (00 44) **0116 234 0205**

CONVALESCENT HEART

Lynne Collins

They called Romily the Snow Queen, but once she had been all fire and passion, kindled into loving by a man's kiss and sure it would last a lifetime. She still believed it would, for her. It had lasted only a few months for the man who had stormed into her heart. After Greg, how could she trust any man again? So was it likely that surgeon Jake Conway could pierce the icy armour that the lovely ward sister had wrapped about her emotions?

TOO MANY LOVES

Juliet Gray

Justin Caldwell, a famous personality of stage and screen, was blessed with good looks and charm that few women could resist. Stacy was a newcomer to England and she was not impressed by the handsome stranger; she thought him arrogant, ill-mannered and detestable. By the time that Justin desired to begin again on a new footing it was much too late to redeem himself in her eyes, for there had been too many loves in his life.

MYSTERY AT MELBECK

Gillian Kaye

Meg Bowering goes to Melbeck House in the Yorkshire Dales to nurse the rich, elderly Mrs Peacock. She likes her patient and is immediately attracted to Mrs Peacock's nephew and heir, Geoffrey, who farms nearby. But Geoffrey is a gambling man and Meg could never have foreseen the dreadful chain of events which follow. Throughout her ordeal, she is helped by the local vicar, Andrew Sheratt, and she soon discovers where her heart really lies.

HEART UNDER SIEGE

Joy St Clair

Gemma had no interest in men — which was how she had acquired the job of companion/secretary to Mrs Prescott in Kentucky. The old lady had stipulated that she wanted someone who would not want to rush off and get married. But why was the infuriating Shade Lambert so sceptical about it? Gemma was determined to prove to him that she meant what she said about remaining single — but all she proved was that she was far from immune to his devastating attraction!